Hunter

Melissa Hosack

Whimsical Publications, LLC

Florida

To purchase the authorized electronic edition of *Hunter*, visit
www.whimsicalpublications.com

Cover art by John McAllister
Editing by John McAllister

Published in the United States by
Whimsical Publications, LLC
Florida

ISBN-13: 978-1-936167-39-5

Printed in the United States of America

At this moment, when she was trying her best to keep Hans distracted, the exact opposite happened.

Her cell phone trilled loudly, completely throwing *her* off. She glanced down at the noisy electronic device where it sat attached snugly against her hip. The call was from Colton, her best friend and partner. He wouldn't be calling if it weren't an emergency. That didn't make his timing any less horrible. Angrily jabbing the button that would put him on speaker phone, she snapped, "What?"

This lack of focus seemed to anger Hans even more. With an enraged howl, he charged. He ran across the floor in a grotesque imitation of a canine. His clawed hands scraped across the tiling, and he made the snorting sound of a large, wild beast.

Before Gwen could react, he tackled her. They both went down in a tangled mess. She felt coarse fur scratch across her face and saliva drip down her arm. She shoved her elbow out, connecting with his jaw, stopping him a moment before his deadly incisors dug into her shoulder.

"Bitch," Hans snarled, his teeth gnashing at the air in an attempt to injure her in any way he could. "Kill...you..." he grunted, his voice sounding like something out of a nightmare.

Colton's voice interjected itself into their struggle. "Is everything okay there?" he asked in concern. "You sound..." He trailed off, apparently at a lack of words to describe the noises emitting from her end of the line.

"Like I'm in the middle of a brutal fist fight? Imagine that, because I am." Her knee shot upward, and Gwen was pretty sure she connected with the werewolf's groin.

When Hans grunted and released her, Gwen knew she'd been right. He rolled away, wheezing in agony and cradling his man parts.

"I should call back later." Colton's voice could barely be heard over the grunting werewolf. "This is a bad time."

"No," Gwen gasped breathlessly as she struggled to her knees. "This is the perfect time. Not busy at all." She tried to get to her feet, but her boot slipped on the floor. She stumbled, but luckily caught herself on her hands. Taking a deep, calming breath, she lunged to her feet.

"Talk to me. What's so important that you felt the need to call me in the middle of a fight?" She knew there was no way Colton could have known she'd be in a fight at this exact moment, but she gave the snarky comment for the fun of it. As she spoke, she managed to get behind Hans. Before he could stop her, Gwen grabbed the werewolf's head in the crook of her arm.

Hans' eyes widened in horror when he realized what she was about to do. He didn't have time to even attempt to protect himself before she yanked viciously. Bones snapped, and muscles tore.

Breathing heavily, Gwen dropped Hans' body to the ground at her feet. "Case closed," she panted. "Just tell me what's going on already."

"Alright then," Colton said briskly. "I've got some really bad news."

"Always," Gwen accused, wiping sweat away from her brow. "Hit me with it."

"Jared Wilson's daughter has been kidnapped. The local werewolf pack found out he was slipping us information, and they took offense."

If her heart beat, Gwen's would have stopped at that statement. "What?" she gasped in fear. "When?" Her life was always one threat after another, but she didn't like it rubbing off on the few friends she had.

"Just a few hours ago. Jared called me right away." Colton paused, and Gwen could practically hear the gears turning in his head. "One of the cases you're working on involves one of the werewolves from the pack involved. If you can find Hans, we can perhaps question him."

Gwen looked down at the body at her feet in disbelief. Of all the rotten timing... "Um," she started, not wanting to admit she'd just killed the man they needed to help them.

Acknowledgements

I would like to dedicate this book to all of the supportive men in my life. To Adam and Mikey, the true masters of the Midnight Wendys Run. Thank you for buying everything I throw out there. Your support is invaluable. To Brian "Brynna" for allowing me to run Team Bruiser even though it is named after you. To my husband Jeremy for reading and editing everything I write with such attentiveness before I even think about sending it out to anyone. And lastly, to the newest man in my life, baby Marshall Frost Hosack. Beware of the level 5s little man!

Prologue

Gwendolyn Fox was in the most vicious battle of her life...okay, 'most vicious battle of her life' might be a bit of an exaggeration, but she was definitely in the most vicious battle of her week.

Most people, when coming face to face with a really pissed off vampire, quickly surrendered with their tail tucked between their legs. Not werewolves though. Of course, one of the only groups in town to actually *have* tails didn't tuck them and run. Instead, they growled and slobbered...and gave you a right hook to the jaw when you approached.

As the burly, hairy half-man took another swing at her, Gwen was barely able to duck underneath his massive arm. "Don't you think this is a bit extreme?" she asked as she made sure to avoid the dangerous claws at the end of his no longer human hands. "I just want to talk."

His response was a ferocious growl. Spittle flew from between his maw, dribbling along a set of sharp teeth. His breath was fetid, his teeth covered in plaque. He was disgusting in every sense of the word.

"Now I know you guys can talk while in wolf form," Gwen wheedled. "It may sound like you've been gargling glass, but at least it's an attempt at being domesticated. How about we talk this out?" She knew her insult on his speaking abilities would only piss him off more, but she wasn't really looking for a conversation. She was just trying to keep him distracted while she looked for an opening.

This was her job, protecting members lower on the supernatural food chain from those bigger and badder than themselves. As jobs went, it was pretty grueling. There wasn't even any hazard pay. Hell, sometimes she was lucky to get paid at all. It worked for her though. Being a vampire, a 9 to 5 job wasn't really in the cards. Plus, she'd get bored behind an office desk.

Not only was her job a pain in the ass, it was a pretty thankless one as well. No one really knew how many threats she kept out of the general population. "Ungrateful people. I put myself in danger for you guys, and do I even get a 'thank you'? Of course not," she whispered to herself as the werewolf let out another roar of rage. Apparently, she'd interrupted his dinner.

His 'dinner', a four-year-old blond girl with pigtails, was cowering in the corner. Her blue eyes were wide, and her gaze flitted back and forth between Gwen and the werewolf.

When the little girl gave a squeak of fear, the werewolf became distracted. He hesitated, his eyes flicking toward her. Next, his massive head whipped in the girl's direction, and his nostrils flared. He gave a snort, his yellow eyes perusing the girl as if she were a menu.

This gave Gwen an opening. Moving quickly, she lifted a booted foot and kicked the werewolf in the chest.

He stumbled back, trying to regain his footing, not an easy feat when you're no more than a dog standing upright.

"Hey, Hans," Gwen said conversationally as she spun, kicking him once again in the chest, "does Mario know you're chowing down on little kids?"

Mario Cessarini was the leader of the local werewolf pack. He was a notorious thug who took pleasure in terrorizing anyone weaker than himself. Hell, he even victimized the lower members in his pack whenever he grew bored of the rest of the world. Mario was all about torture and misery.

"Of course he knows," Gwen answered her own question in disgust. "He's probably encouraging you." She gave the werewolf a third kick to the ribs. With satisfaction, she heard a few break as he finally fell to the ground.

"Hans," she said, repeating his name to ensure he knew there was no way for him to remain anonymous, "have you not read the story of *Little Red Riding Hood*? I suppose not. Mario's muscle men aren't known for being bright. You would need to learn how to read first," she taunted.

The snarl he gave her in response shook the walls of the run down shack he called home.

"Let me fill you in on how the story ends." She attempted to circle around him, each step taken with extreme caution. "A bunch of hunters get together and shoot the big bad wolf. Boom! He dies. Roll end credits."

At this moment, when she was trying her best to keep Hans distracted, the exact opposite happened. Her cell phone trilled loudly, completely throwing *her* off. She glanced down at the noisy electronic device where it sat attached snugly against her hip. The call was from Colton, her best friend and partner. He wouldn't be calling if it weren't an emergency. That didn't make his timing any less horrible. Angrily jabbing the button that would put him on speaker phone, she snapped, "What?"

This lack of focus seemed to anger Hans even more. With an enraged howl, he charged. He ran across the floor in a grotesque imitation of a canine. His clawed hands scraped across the tiling, and he made the snorting sound of a large, wild beast.

Before Gwen could react, he tackled her. They both went down in a tangled mess. She felt coarse fur scratch across her face and saliva drip down her arm. She shoved her elbow out, connecting with his jaw, stopping him a moment before his deadly incisors dug into her shoulder.

"Bitch," Hans snarled, his teeth gnashing at the air in an attempt to injure her in any way he could. "Kill...you..." he grunted, his voice sounding like something out of a nightmare.

Colton's voice interjected itself into their struggle. "Is everything okay there?" he asked in concern. "You sound..." He trailed off, apparently at a lack of words to describe the noises emitting from her end of the line.

"Like I'm in the middle of a brutal fist fight? Imagine that, because I am." Her knee shot upward, and Gwen was pretty sure she connected with the werewolf's groin.

When Hans grunted and released her, Gwen knew she'd been right. He rolled away, wheezing in agony and cradling his man parts.

"I should call back later." Colton's voice could barely be heard over the grunting werewolf. "This is a bad time."

"No," Gwen gasped breathlessly as she struggled to her

knees. "This is the perfect time. Not busy at all." She tried to get to her feet, but her boot slipped on the floor. She stumbled, but luckily caught herself on her hands. Taking a deep, calming breath, she lunged to her feet.

"Talk to me. What's so important that you felt the need to call me in the middle of a fight?" She knew there was no way Colton could have known she'd be in a fight at this exact moment, but she gave the snarky comment for the fun of it. As she spoke, she managed to get behind Hans. Before he could stop her, Gwen grabbed the werewolf's head in the crook of her arm.

Hans' eyes widened in horror when he realized what she was about to do. He didn't have time to even attempt to protect himself before she yanked viciously. Bones snapped, and muscles tore.

Breathing heavily, Gwen dropped Hans' body to the ground at her feet. "Case closed," she panted. "Just tell me what's going on already."

"Alright then," Colton said briskly. "I've got some really bad news."

"Always," Gwen accused, wiping sweat away from her brow. "Hit me with it."

"Jared Wilson's daughter has been kidnapped. The local werewolf pack found out he was slipping us information, and they took offense."

If her heart beat, Gwen's would have stopped at that statement. "What?" she gasped in fear. "When?" Her life was always one threat after another, but she didn't like it rubbing off on the few friends she had.

"Just a few hours ago. Jared called me right away." Colton paused, and Gwen could practically hear the gears turning in his head. "One of the cases you're working on involves one of the werewolves from the pack involved. If you can find Hans, we can perhaps question him."

Gwen looked down at the body at her feet in disbelief. Of all the rotten timing... "Um," she started, not wanting to admit she'd just killed the man they needed to help them.

"You just killed him, didn't you?" Colton asked dully.

"Yep," she came back, her voice full of irony.

"Wonderful," he grumbled. "Did you at least save the little elf girl?"

Gwen glanced at the tiny girl quivering in the corner.

"Yeah. At least one good thing came from all of this." With a sigh, she shook her head at their luck. "I'll take her home and meet back up with you at the apartment building. We'll figure something out."

"I'll work on things from my end," Colton promised. "See you in a few."

"See you," Gwen said almost numbly as she disconnected. Her gaze lowered to the dead werewolf. "Son of a bitch," she grumbled. She let her head fall back, her hair cascading behind her as she fought not to lose her temper. Even in death, Hans had bested her. Letting her breath out in a huff, she straightened and looked at the little elf girl. "Ready to go home?"

Instead of joy and gratitude, the girl glared at her. "You killed him. You're a very bad woman." Indignantly, the girl marched out of the room.

Gwen's jaw dropped, and she stared after the pigtailed child. "He was going to eat you!" she hollered at the pink-clad, retreating child. "You were his dinner!" When it became apparent that the girl wasn't listening, Gwen sighed again. "I hate elves," she snarled before following after the four-year-old spitfire.

Chapter 1

Gwendolyn Fox glared at her oldest friend in the world, Colton Abrams. She crossed her arms defiantly over her chest and said, "I don't work with elves."

Gwen was a force to be reckoned with even if she was petite. At 5'10", she was tall for a woman, but her bone structure was delicate. She had a tiny waist, tiny feet, and tiny hands. Being a vampire, she didn't let her size hinder her. She could tip over a Buick with one hand and not even work up a sweat.

True to vampire legend, her skin was pale, looking almost sickly when she got under bright lighting. She had stunning blue eyes and black hair that hung nearly to her waist. She was beautiful, but put more effort into her attitude than her appearance. The last thing she was going to do was take crap from someone because they assumed beautiful meant weak.

Colton set his face in determined resolve. "He's the only person to ever break into Mario Cessarini's place and live to tell the tale. I've been told he's an expert on breaking into places that are virtually impenetrable. He's supposed to be the best. We need him."

Gwen sighed. This conversation had been going in circles for the past hour. "We don't need him. He's obviously not very intelligent by the fact that he even attempted to break into Mario's place. He probably only got out by dumb luck."

"It's your job to find out whether this guy is the real deal or not. You're going." At 6'4" and built like a linebacker,

Colton was pretty intimidating. He was African American. His skin was the color of milk chocolate, all smooth and warm looking. His hair was done in tidy cornrows that brushed the back of his neck. His hazel eyes held steadily to hers, letting her know there was no room for debate.

Too bad Gwen had been friends with him too long to be affected by his gruff appearance. "But—"

"No buts, Gwenny. Mario has Wilson's daughter."

Gwen frowned at the nickname, but also at his statement. Jared Wilson was a local doctor, a human. She and Colton considered him to be their only mortal friend.

She and Colton made their livings as something similar to what humans referred to as bounty hunters. They tracked down members of the supernatural community that decided laws didn't pertain to them. They'd been working together longer than Gwen could remember.

A few years back, Colton had gotten into a bad motorcycle accident. He'd been in pursuit of a witch who was using black magic to do physical harm to her ex-husband.

The witch had sent a shot of that black magic out her car window to collide with Colton when he started gaining on her little foreign car with his motorcycle. This caused Colton's bike to skid. He was thrown to the opposite side of the road into oncoming traffic. Before its driver could stop, a semi truck ran him over, crushing him under at least half a dozen tires.

Paramedics had pronounced Colton dead at the crash scene. The lack of a pulse and the fact that he'd been pulverized by a semi was all the proof they'd needed.

Colton had awoken on a gurney as he was being wheeled down to the morgue.

Instead of screaming like a girl and bolting at the sound of a dead man's groans, Dr. Jared Wilson had helped Colton. He wasn't freaked out by Colton's request for blood or his continued lack of a heartbeat. Jared had taken the news of the vampire virus in stride. He'd kept Colton hidden until Gwen could get to the hospital to take her friend home. Since that night, Jared had been contacting them anytime something paranormal ran across his path.

Apparently the evil members of the supernatural community didn't take kindly to being ratted out by a human.

Notorious thug and werewolf, Mario Cessarini, had taken

Jared's eleven-year-old daughter, Marla, as retribution. It was up to the good guys to get her back...if she was even still alive that is.

Gwen sighed again, relenting to Colton's demands. "Alright," she huffed, "but I'm doing this for Wilson, not because you told me to."

Colton grinned. "Of course." He tried to keep the amusement over her assurance that she wasn't doing this to please him out of his voice. She always had some ulterior motive to give him to explain why she was doing him a favor. Heaven forbid the rest of the world find out she had a soft side. "The elf's name is Hunter Price," he said, trying not to sound smug at her compliance. "I was told I could find him at an auto repair shop at 1594 Grant Street."

Gwen brushed her long, dark hair out of her eyes as she made a quick check of her weaponry. "You know," she said, "*you* could go get the elf just as easily."

Colton let out a low, deep chuckle. "Your presence will be better accepted than mine."

While loading a fresh clip into her handgun, Gwen looked up in surprise. "Me? I'm the last person an elf—" She broke off with a gasp. "Are you implying that because you're black, he would be suspicious of your motives?"

"No," Colton said, rolling his eyes. "The elf will probably like you better, because I'm an imposing dude who could whoop his ass, and you're a cute, fragile girl with a nice looking backside."

Gwen scowled, sliding the gun into a shoulder holster hidden behind her jacket. "I could kick his ass too, and I'm not fragile."

"Yeah, but he won't know any of that," Colton argued, "and he's not going to either." His voice held a threatening warning at the second half of his sentence. The last thing they needed was for Gwen to bully someone they needed help from. "Just pick the guy up and bring him here. I'll deal with him after that."

"Can't I just knock him around a little bit?" Gwen wheedled.

Colton gave her a scolding look. "Gwenny," he warned.

"Just a bloody nose? One little whack in the face?"

"Gwen! We want this guy to help us. If you bloody him up, he's going to clam up," Colton explained patiently.

"Or I'll terrorize him into spilling everything he knows. Elves are notorious sissies."

"Gwen!" Colton admonished. "Play nice. We'll try the polite approach first."

Gwen shook her head in disappointment. "Alright," she grumbled. "I'll do things your way...until he gives me lip."

Colton sighed, but he gave her some leeway. "Fine. If he gives you any crap, you can...*convince* him to cooperate."

Gwen beamed at him. "I'm suddenly looking forward to this trip." With that, she walked purposefully from the room.

"Gwen!" Colton yelled after her in warning.

Gwen smiled wickedly, ignoring her friend's admonishment. She was definitely looking forward to this trip if there was a possibility of roughing up a poor, unsuspecting elf.

Chapter 2

Gwen marched into the small auto repair shop Colton had given her the address to. Her nose curled up in disgust at the smell of sweat and grease. "Hello!" she called out, booted heels clicking against the cement floor.

No one responded, but Gwen could see someone bent over the engine of a car. "Hello," she said again in annoyance at having to repeat herself. She strode closer, head held high with confidence, but her steps faltered as her eyes landed on the nicest ass she'd ever seen. Whatever she'd been about to say came out a garbled mess.

The man whose backside she was eyeing straightened and spun to face her, cleaning his hands on a dirty rag. "Can I help you?" he asked pleasantly.

Gwen stared at him in stunned silence. In front of her stood the most attractive man she'd ever seen. He was her type if any man in existence ever was.

He was tall, skinny, and had the most startling green eyes. Long, shoulder length brown hair skimmed a nice set of shoulders that tapered down to a narrow waist. His arms were muscled without going overboard. He wouldn't ever be mistaken for a bodybuilder, but he was in good enough shape to warrant a second glance...or a fourth.

Gwen blinked at him, trying to switch her mind away from carnal acts to the business she'd come here for. "Um," she said, shaking her head to clear it. "I'm looking for a Hunter Price. I was told I could find him here."

The man smiled, leaning back against the car, elbows

resting on the frame. "I'm Hunter," he said with an easy smile. "Looks like you found me."

"You're...wait. You can't be. That's impossible. You look..." She trailed off, unable to find the words to depict what she was trying to say.

Hunter raised one thin eyebrow. "Like Saul from Pineapple Express, only taller and better looking?" he offered.

Gwen blinked again, not following him. "What?" Her brain felt fuzzy. It was having a hard time wrapping itself around the concept that the gorgeous man in front of her was the elf she'd been sent to find.

"The movie? Pineapple Express? Saul? Played by James Franco?" Hunter offered, trying to spark some sense of recognition.

"I've never seen it," Gwen said, her expression puzzled.

"Oh, well you should. It's a good movie. The fact that I totally look like one of the characters makes it all the more entertaining too." He stared at her for a moment, waiting for her to finish her original thought. Obviously, it hadn't had anything to do with James Franco. When she didn't say anything, he finally said, "So..." He drawled the word out slowly. "I look..."

"Nothing like an elf!" Gwen blurted.

Hunter grinned lazily, not at all perturbed that she was aware of his heritage. "I've been told that."

Gwen pressed on, unable to get over the shock of his appearance. "Elves are supposed to be blond and pale and fragile...and they don't do manly things like repair cars."

"Hmm," Hunter said thoughtfully. "I suppose I should look into selling the place then." A wicked grin spread across his face. "Consider this as me officially tendering my resignation...to myself that is." His eyes danced in amusement as he pulled a pack of cigarettes from his back pocket. He tilted the pack until a cigarette came loose and he was able to put it between his lips. Putting the pack back in his pocket, he pulled out a lighter.

Gwen watched in disbelief as Hunter lit up, tendrils of smoke curling up around his head. "You smoke?" she squeaked in horror.

Hunter's head stayed bent over his lighter, but his eyes lifted to hers. "That bother you?"

"It's just...elves don't smoke! You guys are all about being healthy and protecting the environment."

Hunter's lip quirked. "You don't say." He stared at her for a moment before dropping the cigarette to the ground and squashing it under his boot as if to please her. Pushing away from the car, he walked toward Gwen, circling her slowly. "You seem to know an awful lot about what I am, and I don't know a thing about you." He came to a stop in front of her, tilting his head to the side inquisitively.

Gwen tensed as Hunter circled her, feeling her hair shift as he moved the air around her. When he came to stand in front of her, she wet her lips and said softly, "My name's Gwen. Gwendolyn Fox."

"And what are you, sweetheart?" he asked quietly as he lifted a lock of her hair with his fingertips, running the silky strands through his fingers. "You aren't human. I know that much."

Gwen's breath caught in her throat, and she barely managed to say, "I'm a vampire."

"Hmm," Hunter said thoughtfully. "And what's a vampire doing tracking down an elf? It's common knowledge that vampires and elves don't mesh well. You guys are notorious for your superiority complexes when it comes to us."

"Superiority complexes?" Gwen sputtered in disbelief. "It's not a complex if it's the truth...and it's not our fault you guys break so easily."

Hunter's expression turned sour. "If you're looking to ask me a favor, you're going about it the wrong way."

Gwen cross her arms and stared daggers at him. She was beginning to think he was annoying, and now that she could see him up close, or perhaps it was because she now knew he was an elf, he didn't look quite so perfect.

His nose was slightly crooked as if someone had broken it, his hair was slightly tangled, and he had car sludge under his fingernails.

"Your nose is crooked," Gwen said haughtily.

Hunter's eyebrows rose in disbelief. "If you were trying to make things better, you just failed miserably."

Gwen breathed out slowly and forced her arms down to her sides. She plastered a pleasant expression on her face. "I need assistance that requires your expertise," she finally managed to say with only a hint of hostility in her voice.

"It's not polite to just come out and ask for oral sex from

someone you've only just met," Hunter admonished playfully.

Gwen stared at him in utter shock, a small squeak escaping her lips. She didn't know what to say to that.

Hunter gave an amused chuckle. "I'm only messing with you. Man, vampires have absolutely no sense of humor."

Gwen just glared at him.

With a sigh, Hunter gave up. "Alright. I'm done attempting to make nice. What do you want from me? I'm guessing it's not to get enjoyment out of my humor," he added dryly.

"My colleague wishes to discuss hiring you to assist him for a job," Gwen said, her face void of emotion. "He said to tell you to prepare to be gone at least a few days."

"You going to tell me for what?" Hunter asked. On her continued silence, he huffed, "You can't expect me to take off with you for days without giving me any information."

Gwen shifted her weight, avoiding eye contact before finally relenting. "Some bad people kidnapped an innocent little girl. My colleague has confidence that you can help rescue her."

The tone of her voice must have given away her lack of confidence in him, because Hunter said, "But you don't." It wasn't a question. He didn't need to ask because he already knew the answer.

"No, I don't," Gwen admitted, her honesty brutal. "I think you're a nobody who happened to get lucky a few times. I believe your reputation is mostly hype. I think if we employ you, you'll end up getting us all killed."

"That's a good way to win me over," Hunter grumbled sarcastically. To Gwen, he said, "What makes your colleague think I have experience with any of this?"

Gwen's blue eyes lifted to his. "He's heard that you're good with the breaking and entering stuff. You can get past security systems. We need you to get us into the building where they're holding the girl."

Hunter stayed silent. He didn't confirm her statement about him being experienced in getting around security systems, but he didn't deny it either.

Gwen watched Hunter closely as she continued. "You're the only person to ever come out of Mario Cessarini's place alive. We need you to do it again."

Hunter paled visibly, and he took a small step away from

her. The easygoing expression had vacated his face in an instant. "Mario Cessarini?" he asked with a gulp.

Taking in his reaction, Gwen sighed. "I knew this trip was a waste of time," she said almost accusingly. "You can't get us in any better than anyone else."

Hunter's eyes flashed in self-righteousness at the sound of disappointment in her voice. "I didn't say I couldn't do the job. It's just not going to be easy."

Eyebrows rising in surprise, Gwen asked, "So you'll do it then?"

Hunter stared at her for a moment in silence, weighing his options. "How much you paying?" he asked curiously.

"Enough," Gwen snapped in annoyance at his greed. "Don't worry. It'll be worth your while."

Hunter stared at her thoughtfully for a few moments before finally saying, "Alright. I'll do it." The grimace on his face stated that his pride outweighed his self-preservation and common sense.

Not wanting to linger on his poor decision making, Hunter continued to rush blindly into the situation. "I've just got to stop by my place and grab a few things." He looked down at his grease stained hands. "I should probably shower too."

Gwen's eyes narrowed in irritation at the unplanned detour, but she supposed she couldn't expect him to go without at least packing some personal belongings. "Whatever. Just make it quick. The longer you take, the more likely it is that a child dies."

That statement sobered Hunter. He grabbed a set of keys to lock up his garage. "I'll be quick," he promised.

Without needing to say anything else, both of them headed briskly to the doors, their actions motivated by the combined goal to keep a little girl from being murdered.

Chapter 3

When Hunter opened the door to the bathroom in his apartment, Gwen pushed brusquely past him, her eyes scanning the interior with suspicion. She stood in the center of the room with her hands on her hips, lips pursed thoughtfully.

Hunter raised an eyebrow in surprise as he was nearly run into the doorframe. "Sure. Come on in," he said sarcastically. "What are you doing by the way? Making sure you approve of my decor? Looking for shower mold? Or do you just have to pee that badly?"

Gwen shot him a dirty look over her shoulder as she marched over to the single window in the room. "I'm looking for escape routes."

Hunter's eyes clouded with worry. "You think we might get attacked already?" he asked in concern.

"No," Gwen answered distractedly as she fiddled with the locks on the window. "I'm making sure you don't sneak off instead of getting in the shower."

Hunter's eyes widened at her comment. "Good God, woman. Show a little trust. If I was planning on trying to make an escape, I wouldn't have let you know where I live. I'd have just declined your offer to begin with or made a break for it on the walk over here."

"I saw the thought cross your mind a couple times," Gwen pointed out. "At one point I thought I was going to have to knock you unconscious and drag you the rest of the way."

The tips of Hunter's ears, which were adorably pointed, turned red in embarrassment at the fact that she'd noticed his fleeting moments of cowardice. His delicate green eyes had also widened in horror. "Would it really have been necessary to bludgeon me over the head like a caveman and drag me home?"

Gwen smiled cutely up at him as she squeezed passed him out of the bathroom and into his connecting bedroom. "Necessary, no. Fun, yes." She plopped down on the edge of his bed, crossing her legs and arms impatiently. "There's no way to escape from your bathroom. You are free to wash up. Make it quick. I want to get out of here."

Hunter narrowed his eyes as he shut the door on her, mumbling, "Why thank you for the permission to use my own bathroom."

Gwen only rolled her eyes in response. She waited until she heard the shower start up before looking thoughtfully around his bedroom. She looked for signs of what his personality was like, what his hobbies were. She desperately wanted to know if she could trust Hunter. She tried to convince herself that she was only curious because they had business together and not because she was interested in him. The business aspect was enough for her to worry about. It was shaky at best. Elves and vampires didn't have good track records of working together.

Elves automatically translated *vampire* into evil. That wasn't always the case. In fact, she'd run across a couple elves that were downright evil with a capital E. They didn't all make cookies or fill Santa's sleigh like most people pictured them doing. Some of them did dark magic, magic so black it tainted the soul, stealing little bits of humanity away with each use.

Of course, when the dust cleared after she'd battled such vicious killers, whose side did people want to take, a poor dead elf or the evil vampire who killed said elf? That's right, the elf.

With a little huff of annoyance, Gwen slid open a drawer of the nightstand next to the bed. All she found inside were stray coins, expired coupons, a few other odds and ends, and... Gwen blinked. Hair barrettes? The man clipped his hair back with a barrette? She wasn't sure whether she found that to be cute or appalling. Sliding the drawer shut, she rolled onto her stomach and lifted the draping blanket to look underneath the bed.

Under the bed lay a dusty pair of rollerblades. Elves on wheels? That didn't sound like a safe combination. Elves broke way too easily.

She was so busy snooping around under Hunter's bed that she wasn't paying attention to the rest of the room. Something suddenly landed on her back, and Gwen gave a yelp of surprise.

Ignoring her startled cry, the thing on her back began purring and kneading its paws against the back of her shirt.

A cat? Hunter had a cat? Lying frozen, Gwen was half afraid to move. Of course he would have a cat. Vampire hunters not included, what hated vampires just as much as elves? Cats.

Feeling silly for her anxiety, it was just a stupid cat after all, Gwen rolled onto her side.

The cat slid off to lie next to her.

Rolling to face the animal, Gwen eyed the cat suspiciously as if she expected it to attack her.

The little black fluff ball just peered up at her with big eyes. Giving a little yawn, it stretched out one of its tiny paws to touch her hand.

Surprised, Gwen shifted her hand to scratch under the cat's chin. "You're a cute little thing," she observed.

"She's too friendly for her own good," Hunter's voice interrupted.

Gwen's eyes lifted, and she found him leaning against the doorframe that connected the bathroom to the bedroom with an unreadable look on his face.

He was wearing nothing but a towel slung low on his hips. Beads of water trailed slowly down his tanned chest.

Gwen kept her eyes carefully trained on the kitten. "She's black," she said haughtily. "A supernatural being such as yourself owning a black cat? Don't you find that to be a bit stereotypical?"

Hunter shrugged. "No human family wanted her because she was black, and they were superstitious. I couldn't leave her to be adopted by a practitioner of the black arts. She's got too nice of a personality. She's too innocent for that garbage."

Gwen's eyes lifted to Hunter in surprise. "You could sense

her personality?" She knew that elves were born with the mystical gift of reading people. They were a tricky group to deceive because they had the ability to instantly know how a certain person will react in a situation. They were psychics of the personality. She knew of their talent to instantly read people, but animals?

Hunter strode over to the dresser against the far wall. "Sure I can."

"And she's got a friendly personality?" Gwen asked, twirling a finger around the kitten's tail.

"Her name is Zoey, and yes." With that, Hunter grabbed the knot in his towel and released it. The towel slid unceremoniously to the floor.

Gwen gawked in disbelief. One minute she'd been simply talking to a man in a towel. It was a little unsettling, but nothing she couldn't handle. Now, she was seeing all of Hunter, and she meant *all*. With a squeak of protest, Gwen asked, "What are you doing?!"

"Getting dressed," Hunter said casually as he turned his back on her and began rummaging through a drawer. "You're so untrusting that I figured I'd keep myself in your sight as much as possible."

And boy, are you in my sight, Gwen thought as her eyes strayed to his fabulous backside. For the intent of keeping him aware of how serious their situation was, she said in her most stern voice, "You're going way overboard, and you know it."

Shrugging into a pair of boxer shorts, Hunter gave her an accusing look. "*I'm* going overboard? Why don't you take a look in the mirror, sweet cheeks? Oh wait!" he cried, snapping his fingers. "You can't, because you have no reflection. It must be such a challenge to do your hair in the mornings."

"I do have a reflection!" Gwen cried defensively, feeling insulted. "That whole thing about vampires casting no reflection is just a stupid myth...and *your* hair was a mess earlier. What's your excuse?"

Hunter's hair had been messy at best before his shower. Now it was smoothed back and slick looking.

"I didn't realize I was supposed to look like a supermodel while repairing cars," Hunter said dryly as he yanked a pair of pants from a laundry basket of unfolded clothes. Sliding one foot into them, he hopped around in an attempt to tug them up. "We all don't walk around wearing skintight leather pants." His eyes narrowed accusingly. "And who are you to talk about my cat being stereotypical? You're a walking stereotype! You're a vampire in leather pants just oozing sexuality while you sulk around in your own personal cloud of gloom."

Gwen looked down at her pants, affronted. Then something he said caught her attention. "You think I ooze sexuality?" She almost snarled at the feeling of a blush creeping up her cheeks. Damn it. Why was she such a spaz when men were involved? A couple hundred years of living, and she'd still never learned to deal with the opposite sex.

Hunter snorted as he pulled a t-shirt over his head, effectively mussing his hair. "Honey, you're lounging on my bed looking fine as hell in those ass-kicking boots. I hate vampires, and I would do unimaginably dirty things to you if I didn't think you'd kick my ass for it."

Gwen broke into a fit of coughing at his statement. "That's right I would," she said hoarsely, clearing her throat. Yeah, she looked like a real badass choking on air.

"Pity," Hunter said, eyeing her chest almost regretfully. "It could have been fun." He gave a shrug. "Ah well." With that, he began packing an overnight bag.

Gwen watched as he shoved a handful of socks into the bag, trying to think of a way to once again have the upper hand. Finally, she settled on embarrassing him like he'd done to her. "Don't forget to pack your barrettes," she said tauntingly.

"Oh, thank you," Hunter said, not embarrassed in the least. He walked to the bedside drawer and began plucking a few barrettes free of stray coupons and paperclips. Suddenly, he froze as something hit him. His eyes lifted to Gwen, and he tried to ignore how good she looked sprawled out on his bed with Zoey curled against her side. "You looked through my stuff?" he said in surprise. Then, as that thought settled in, his shoulders relaxed, and he lifted a barrette to clip his hair back. "Typical vampire." His voice didn't sound mad at all. In fact, he seemed to accept her snooping pretty easily.

Gwen on the other hand couldn't accept his response to her snooping. Trying to get a reaction out of him, she said, "I saw the roller blades under the bed too." She lifted her chin almost challengingly.

"Awesome," Hunter said distractedly as he made his way toward the bathroom to grab his toiletries. "Then I'm sure you saw all the naughty sex toys in the back of my closet." He paused in the bathroom doorway. "I'm going back in here for a few minutes to pack a few necessities. Don't worry. I'm not bolting."

As he disappeared from view, Gwen shot the closet a curious look. *Sex toys?* She glanced toward the bathroom doorway then back to the closet. *What the hell,* she decided. Hunter was preoccupied in the bathroom for the time being. It wouldn't hurt to satisfy her curiosity. Climbing to her feet, Gwen tiptoed to the closet and slid back the door.

Inside were neat rows of dress shirts, a few boxes of shoes, and a rack of ties. Apparently, Mr. Mechanic didn't mind dressing nice every once in awhile. Sitting on a shelf was a little wooden box that she thought might hold some naughty interest, but it ended up only being jewelry.

Gwen was just about to give up her search, figuring Hunter would be back soon, when Zoey sauntered into the closet.

The kitten meandered to the back and flopped down on a pile of folded blankets.

"Zoey," Gwen hissed, snapping her fingers at the cat as if that would get her to leave the closet. "Zoey!"

The cat didn't budge. It only purred, content with its pile of soft blankets.

Cursing under her breath, Gwen dropped to her hands and knees. She crawled toward the cat, making soft cooing noises.

"You know," Hunter said from directly behind her, "I was only joking about the sex toys."

Gwen yelped in surprise at his proximity and nearly cracked her head on a shelf. Damn sneaky elves. She hadn't even heard him approaching.

At Gwen's startled cry, Zoey went racing out of the closet and skittered across the floor to disappear under the bed.

Gwen took a deep breath to force away her embarrassment before she climbed to her feet and faced Hunter, hands on her hips. It would have been more threatening, but with him in the doorway to the closet like he was, she was pinned against a row of shirts. "I wasn't snooping," she informed him. "Your cat got in here, and I was trying to shoo her out."

Hunter's lip quirked in amusement. "How'd she get in when the door was closed?"

Finding no way out of her predicament, Gwen snapped, "Fine! You're right. I was nosing about your closet, looking for anything of interest. I didn't find anything though. Frankly, you're pretty boring. I didn't find a single sex toy," she accused.

Reaching to the rack along the wall, Hunter grabbed a green, silk tie. He draped it over her neck, holding tightly to each end. "This is all the sex toy I need," he informed her huskily. He slowly lowered his head over Gwen's upturned face and brushed his lips ever so gently across hers.

Gwen thought she might melt into the floor when Hunter's lips grazed along hers. A mix of adrenaline and fear zipped through her. Panicking, she brought her arm forward and smashed the heel of her palm into Hunter's stomach, effectively knocking the wind out of him.

Hunter wheezed and stumbled backwards, clutching his stomach with both hands. "Damn...vampire," he coughed in pain.

Yanking the tie from around her neck, Gwen tossed it to the floor. "Don't you ever pull that kind of crap with me again," she warned. "Just who the hell do you think you are?"

Hunter's face was bright red. She wasn't sure if it was from the blow to the gut or frustration. It looked like it could possibly be both.

"I don't know why I did that," he said with anger in his tone. "I hate freaking nasty, dead vampires. You're a walking corpse," Hunter accused. His eyes slid to hers, and there was real concern in his expression over his actions. "But damn you smell good. Like jasmine and leather. It's the most erotic thing..." He trailed off, not wanting to continue with that train of thought. "I couldn't stop myself."

Gwen couldn't help but feel insulted at the walking corpse remark, but his compliments helped lessen the sting. She stared at him in uncertainty, afraid to even comment. After a moment, she finally settled on, "We should get going."

Hunter averted his eyes, using picking up his duffle bag as an excuse not to look at her. "Yeah." Clearing his throat uncomfortably, he spun to face Zoey who was peeking out from under the bed. "Come on, Zoe Zoe," he coaxed. "We're gonna take a vacation for a couple of days."

"You're bringing the cat?" Gwen asked derisively.

"Well, I'm certainly not leaving her here alone to starve to death," Hunter came back indignantly.

"Fine," Gwen snapped. "Whatever. Bring the cat." Her tone was harsh, but the sight of Zoey's soft yellowish green eyes peering at her from under the edge of the comforter warmed her heart.

Striding over to the bed, Hunter scooted the kitten up into his arms. Shifting her to the side, he cradled Zoey against his body in the crook of an arm.

Zoey settled in happily, a purr coming from her almost immediately.

Gwen had to admit, they made a cute pair. "You carry her like she's a football," she said with a little laugh.

Hunter turned to face her, his green eyes wide in mock surprise. "Was that a laugh? I must be going crazy, because I swear I just heard a vampire giggle." His free hand went to his heart as if to check if it was still beating. "I think I might be going into shock."

"Go," Gwen demanded, finger pointed at the door. Though her tone was tough, there was a smirk on her lips.

Tossing her a lopsided grin, Hunter bowed his head. "As my vampire bids." With that, he loped through the door, his gangly frame bouncing with each step.

Chapter 4

Gwen stood outside the apartment building she co-owned with Colton. It was four floors, and there were originally four apartments inside, one for each floor. She and Colton had taken the apartment on the bottom floor and turned it into a common kitchen and living room area. Of the other apartments, Gwen had taken the one on the second floor, and Colton lived in the one on the third floor. They kept the fourth floor apartment for guests, not that they'd ever had any. Hunter would be their first guest in, well, ever.

Wringing her hands nervously, Gwen stared up at the building that had been her safe haven for years. "Well, this is it." She was uneasy about anyone new entering her home. She and Colton were safe here, because no one knew where they lived. Inviting a stranger in was like inviting trouble.

"Cool," Hunter said, his voice carefree. He adjusted the duffel bag on his shoulder and stared up at the building. He didn't seem the least bit apprehensive about the fact that he was about to enter a vampire lair.

Gwen shot him a sidelong glance, her trepidation getting the best of her. "When you get inside, don't touch anything," she threatened. "I'm not happy about you waltzing into my life or my home. Please make this easier by not violating my personal space any more than you have to."

"Waltzing in?" Hunter asked in disbelief. "*You* hunted *me* down. You practically took me prisoner." His eyes narrowed slightly. "You expect me to just pack up my life for a few days because it's convenient for you, but I'm not allowed to touch anything in yours? What are you afraid of? That I'll eat the last of your Honey Nut Cheerios?"

"I'm not afraid," Gwen was quick to respond. "I just don't want elf germs all over my things."

"Elf germs!" Hunter cried as she unlocked the front door. When she sashayed into the foyer, he quickly pushed in after her, his expression full of outrage. "Why are you so worried about germs? You're a corpse! You're not going to catch anything from my diseased elf body."

Gwen slammed the door a little harder than she needed to as irritation swelled inside of her. "I want you in my life as little as can be helped. Don't touch anything that belongs to me, especially not my Honey Nut Cheerios! Those definitely aren't for you. Got it?"

When she'd slammed the door, Zoey had lunged out of Hunter's arms and scurried off.

"No," Hunter spat back, agitatedly shaking his hand where Zoey had scratched him in her attempt to get away from the loudness of their argument. "I don't *got it*. I don't get why you're being so weird, particularly about the stupid box of cereal."

"Well, I am," Gwen snapped. "Don't give me crap about it."

Dropping his bag to the hardwood floor, Hunter took a menacing step forward. "I'll give you crap when you're acting like a maniac who doesn't make any sense."

"So you're saying you're going to be difficult?" Gwen asked, eyes lighting up almost as if in delight.

"Yep." Hunter crossed his arms over his chest with a smug smirk. "I plan on being very difficult, more difficult than you could even imagine."

Gwen's mouth curved into a wicked grin. "I see." All of a sudden, she pulled her arm back, brought her fist forward, and punched Hunter in the nose.

He doubled over, clutching his face in pain, but not before she caught his eyes widening in absolute shock. "What was that for?" he mumbled around his hands.

Ignoring him, Gwen strode into the living room, a giant grin on her face. "I'm back!" she called gaily. When Colton looked up from the newspaper he was reading, she said, "He gave me lip."

Colton climbed anxiously to his feet. "Oh, Gwenny. You didn't!"

Hunter took that moment to stumble into the room. He was dabbing at his nose with two fingers, the small trickle of blood coming from his left nostril staining his fingertips. "You hit me," he said in disbelief.

Gwen smirked and leaned against the wall, feeling pretty damn proud of herself.

Colton rushed forward, his tone placating. "I'm terribly sorry, Mr. Pierce. Gwendolyn can be..."

"A vicious bitch?" Hunter supplied.

"Well, yes," Colton admitted, shooting Gwen a reproachful look.

"Hey," Gwen cried, pushing off the wall in agitation. "You said if he gave me crap, I could hit him. He gave me crap. The end result was his own fault."

Hunter's eyes widened. "I...you...you baited me!" He shook his head in incredulity, realizing that arguing with her wasn't going to get him anywhere. "Your attitude defies all logic."

Gwen wanted to stick her tongue out at him, but figured it would seem childish.

Giving his roommate a warning glare, Colton motioned for Hunter to take a seat on the couch. "Once again, my apologies, Mr. Pierce. Had I realized Gwendolyn was going to be so...difficult, I would have gone to get you myself. I was concerned you wouldn't receive me well, though. I've been told my appearance is somewhat intimidating." Realizing he hadn't introduced himself, he added, "I'm Colton by the way, the nicer one of this vampire duo." His eyes slid to Hunter's nose. "Let me go find a towel so you can clean that up." Halfway to the door, he asked, "Would you care for anything else? A drink perhaps?"

"Depends," Hunter said suspiciously. "I know what kind of drink your lot prefers."

"We drink more than blood," Colton assured him while Gwen shot Hunter a look of indignation.

"You got any Dew?" Hunter asked.

"Mountain Dew? Yes, of course," Colton said, oozing hospitality. "Shall I bring you a glass of that?"

Gwen rolled her eyes in annoyance at Colton's placating attitude. He might as well get on his knees and kiss the elf's feet while he was at it.

"That sounds great," Hunter said with an easy smile, pouring on the charm. "Add in a bowl of Honey Nut Cheerios and that would be just about perfect."

Gwen gave an incensed squawk.

In the doorway to the kitchen, Colton froze and gave Hunter a puzzled look. "Honey Nut Cheerios? That's an odd request, but I believe we have some…" He trailed off thoughtfully, wracking his brain on whether they had the cereal or not.

"We don't," Gwen was quick to inform them.

"No…I'm pretty sure we do," Colton said slowly. He was rewarded with a nasty look from Gwen.

"I'm just kidding," Hunter said with a chuckle at Gwen's denial. "Mountain Dew is fine."

As soon as Colton was out of the room, Gwen spun on Hunter. "Real cute, elf boy. I bet you think you're terribly funny."

"I'd rather be funny than insane," Hunter accused. He leaned back in his seat and casually crossed an ankle over his knee.

His casual manner only made her angrier. Gwen moved forward, hands outstretched as if she wanted to choke him. "I'm only acting insane because you've made me this way," she hissed.

Hunter's eyes flicked to her hands before returning to her face. "I haven't made you anything. *You* sought me out. Either send me on my way or act as if you actually want my help."

"I never wanted your help," Gwen spat, coming to stand directly in front of him. "That was all Colton."

"Well, if you don't want Colton upset with you, you'd better learn to play nice." Hunter shifted in his seat in agitation, his foot returning to the floor. "You hit me again, and I walk."

"You have no right to tell me what to do." As if to prove this, Gwen's arms shot out for his throat.

With supernatural reflexes, Hunter intercepted her hands. He shoved them downward, grabbed her wrists, and yanked her roughly toward him.

Gwen tumbled gracelessly into his lap. One of her knees slid between his on the couch, and she collapsed against his chest. The only thing that kept her from cracking her head against his was dumb luck.

Hunter's hands were tight around her wrists, keeping her from getting up. "I'm not joking with you, Gwen. This is going to be dangerous enough without having to worry about you surprise attacking me. You keep this up, and I'll leave.

That little girl will die, and it will be your fault. You understand?"

"I understand," Gwen conceded in frustration. She didn't want to give Hunter the upper hand, but Colton would never forgive her if Marla died because she couldn't be civil to the only man who could help them. Giving in didn't mean she had to suffer the indignity of being sprawled in his lap though.

Gwen struggled against him, her breathing harsh. For an elf, he had a pretty strong grip. As she squirmed, she caught the scent of forest mixed with clean, spring rain. The smell of Hunter's skin was nearly intoxicating. That thought aggravated her even more.

Hunter's lip curled into a wicked grin. "Now that we're on the same page about your violent tendencies, and you're sitting right where I want you, I can stop pretending to be mad." His grip relaxed, becoming more of a caress than a threatening hold.

Gwen gave a soft gasp of disbelief. "You..."

"I was just getting you riled up," he admitted guiltily. "I wouldn't let a little girl die because of your fear of intimate interaction and contact."

"I'm not afraid of..." Gwen trailed off, eyes wide in unease as Hunter lifted a hand and trailed his fingertips along the exposed skin of her shoulder where her shirt had slipped down. Her breath caught in her throat at the hungry look in his eyes.

"Why does it bother you so much that you're attracted to me?" Hunter asked in genuine curiosity.

Lucky for Gwen, she didn't have to answer, because Colton took that moment to return. "Oh dear," he said softly from the doorway.

Gwen panicked. She frantically pushed against Hunter in an attempt to get up. Thankfully, he released his grip on her, and she stumbled clumsily to her feet. "Don't you...I thought I..." She straightened her shirt in embarrassment and shoved her hair away from her face, trying to ignore the way her skin tingled where he'd been touching her. "I hate you," she finally settled with. With graceful strides, she made her way to one of the vacant chairs facing Hunter. It put a coffee table between them, but it didn't remove her from the smoldering look he was sending her.

Colton cleared his throat in discomfort as he handed Hunter a tall glass of Mountain Dew and a towel to mop up the blood from his nose. "Shall we get down to business?" he asked uncertainly as he sunk into the chair next to Gwen's.

It seemed to take an effort, but Hunter dragged his gaze away from Gwen to settle on Colton. "Yes, business." His eyes flicked back to Gwen as he dabbed at his bleeding nose before quickly returning to Colton. "Your associate told me you need me to bypass a security system and help you break into a home."

"Did she tell you which home?" Colton prodded.

Hunter's tan face paled, and he ran a hand nervously through wisps of hair that had come loose from his barrette. "Yeah. She told me which house, more importantly whose." Leaning forward, he braced his elbows on his knees, his head bowed.

Gwen and Colton exchanged a nervous glance at his reaction.

"You won't even have to step inside, Mr. Pierce," Colton assured. "Gwen will be handling that. She's very good at moving around undetected. That's why we work so well together. When we need someone to go in and start busting heads, I'm your guy. Gwen here is the one we use for stealth. Though if things turn violent, she will have no trouble holding her own. Once you get her in, you can leave. All you need to do is get her inside the building and instruct her on how to make it out alive."

After a moment, Hunter's eyes lifted to Colton's and held them. "How much?" he asked softly.

"I'll give you fifty thousand dollars if you provide us with a decent opportunity to get that little girl out alive," Colton said evenly.

Hunter whistled, but didn't speak. He seemed to silently go over their offer, judging whether the profit was worth the risk to his life or not. Finally, he said, "Make it a hundred thousand, and I'm adding the stipulation that I stay with Gwen the entire time."

"Absolutely not!" Gwen cried, lunging to her feet. "I'll have enough problems on my hands without trying to keep a fragile elf alive."

"I can handle myself," Hunter said tensely.

"Apparently not," Gwen shot back. "Seeing as how I broke your nose without much effort at all."

Hunter delicately touched his aching nose. "It's not broken. Besides, I'll be expecting them to do senseless acts of violence. You just caught me off guard because I didn't expect the people asking me for help to attack me so needlessly. Your actions don't seem like a good way to convince me to cooperate."

"No, but a hundred thousand dollars is," Gwen spat in disgust. "A little girl might die, and all you care about is how much profit you can make on the situation."

"If I didn't care about the kid's life, I wouldn't be going in with you," Hunter said through clenched teeth. Before Gwen could argue, he pressed on. "Just because I can get you inside doesn't mean you're home free. There's bound to be security you need my help with that can only be disabled on the inside. Knowing these men, she'll probably be in a locked room. The locks are all going to be number coded. You're going to need someone with knowledge of electronics to get the door open even if you do find her. It's not going to be easy. Hell, I don't know if it's even going to be possible."

Hunter paused. He glanced at Colton before returning his serious gaze to Gwen. "I'm not letting you go in there alone. I know these people. You won't come back out without my help."

"I've been surviving a long time without your help," Gwen said tersely. "I'm sure I'll manage now."

"Why does it bother you so much to admit that you might need my help?" Hunter asked in frustration.

"Why do you-" Gwen started, but Colton cut her off. "Deal," he said, his voice carrying over their argument.

Gwen turned in his direction, astonishment plain on her face. "What?" she screeched.

"He's right, Gwenny. We need him in there," Colton reasoned. "End of discussion."

Hunter snorted. "Did he just call you Gwenny?"

Colton sent Hunter a warning look before continuing with the topic of their rescue plan. "You seem to know the trick of getting into that place. What do you suggest our first step of action should be?"

Hunter shot Gwen one last glance before becoming all business. "The first obstacle is the front gate. The only way to get through is to be buzzed in by the attendant. He's not going to buzz us in without specific instructions from Mr. Cessarini to do so. Going over the fence is a challenge, because we've got motion sensors and security cameras to get around that can only be deactivated from inside the fence. If we could somehow manage to get past those undetected, I could disable them, but it would automatically alert the security guard at the gate that something is up. The guard will come out to investigate why his cameras went dead. Those guards are instructed to shoot first and ask questions later."

"Sounds like fun," Gwen said sarcastically as she leaned back in her seat. She was only playing the part of a stereotypically annoyed vampire, but the look she shot Colton was with genuine concern. This was sounding harder than they'd thought it was going to be.

"There is the back entrance however," Hunter continued. "Only Mario himself and his head security guard Chrispen Winthrow have keys to that gate. They don't like many people to know about the back entrance, so they keep that one less guarded. This is probably our best bet on getting in."

"How do you suggest we get through the back gate?" Colton asked in interest.

The grin that spread across Hunter's face was practically wicked. "Chrispen's going to give the keys to us."

"Unlikely," Gwen argued, "but continue."

"Not unlikely," Hunter corrected. "Chrispen haunts the same overpriced restaurant every Thursday night. It's valet parking. He leaves his keys in the trust of the valets every time. All we have to do is get ahold of them and make a copy. Then we return the keys, and he's none the wiser."

The plan wasn't half bad, but there was one question Gwen felt the need to ask. "If you've done this before, shouldn't you already have a key?"

"For one, that's not exactly how I got in last time, and second, they change the locks every six months. Even if I had a key, it would be useless at this point. It's been almost two years since I broke in."

"For someone who didn't want to go back in, you sure know a lot about what these people are up to," Gwen commented.

"When people have a good reason to possibly want you dead, you keep track of what they're up to," Hunter stated.

Accepting that answer, Colton said, "So we devise a plan to get the keys then."

Gwen nodded, her mind already whirring with possible ideas. "We get the keys."

Chapter 5

Hunter was staring at Gwen with an amused smirk on his face. "Don't you look adorable?" He was trying very hard not to laugh at her obvious discomfort, but it was a challenge he was close to losing.

"Shut up, elf boy," Gwen snarled. She tugged at her skirt in utter mortification. There was nothing she hated more than dressing like a girl, but Hunter had insisted that she needed to look harmless and innocent for this plan to work. So here she was in a tiny blue and black plaid schoolgirl skirt with black knee-high stockings and black buckled flats. Her top was black spandex, the plunge in the neck too low for her comfort. The outfit belonged to Colton's girlfriend, Penelope, making Gwen suddenly curious about what type of games the two of them were playing behind closed doors.

Hunter rolled his eyes at her hostility. "I'm serious. You look...sexy. Why don't you like dressing like a fox?"

"My last name is Fox. That's all the fox I need in my life." Gwen tugged at her top, trying to tuck her cleavage away. "And stop looking at me like that!"

"It's your own fault for totally turning me on," Hunter said huskily.

From seemingly out of nowhere in her skimpy outfit, Gwen produced a gun. She clicked off the safety and aimed it at Hunter's chest.

"That only makes you look hotter," he said on a groan.

Gwen's eyes narrowed. "Not if I shoot you through the heart it won't."

"You wouldn't shoot me," Hunter said with confidence. "You like me far too much to do such a thing."

"Try me," Gwen said dryly. Without another word, she spun and walked away. She tucked the gun into the waistband of her skirt near the small of her back and then covered it with her shirt as she left. Straightening her shoulders, she sashayed purposefully across the street to the teenaged boy who was working the valet service of the restaurant where Chrispen's car was parked. "Excuse me," she said sweetly as she approached.

The kid turned to face her, and his eyes practically bugged out of his head at her appearance. "Can I help you?" he asked, unable or uncaring to hide the eagerness in his voice.

Fighting not to roll her eyes, Gwen tossed him a bright smile. "You sure can!" she gushed. Her hand went to his arm, and she shamelessly batted her eyelashes. "I need a big favor." Her gaze flicked to his nametag. "Stan, today is my cousin's birthday, and I always do something special for him. I need your help with that."

The valet listened with enrapt attention.

Gwen stepped closer to him, her expression friendly and open. "See, my cousin's car is his baby. He loves that thing more than his own mother. What I need is for you to give me the keys so I can have it while he eats his dinner. I'm going to get it washed, waxed, have the tires rotated, have someone give it a tune up...you know, the works. I'll have it back here before he's even served his main course. His girlfriend lent me her key, but I'm a bit absentminded. I forgot it at home. Please help me, Stan. He won't even know you were involved. I promise. He'll think I used his girlfriend's key."

Stan shuffled his feet uncertainly. "We're really not supposed to do that."

Gwen could tell his denial was only halfhearted. He looked as if he was willing to do nearly anything to please her. She pouted, trying to look as girly and unthreatening as possible. "I'm only trying to make Chrispen happy."

Stan choked on his next breath. "Chrispen? Your cousin is Chrispen Winthrow?"

Gwen nodded, widening her eyes innocently. Apparently the Winthrow name didn't just strike fear into the hearts of the supernatural community. They'd been making a reputation with the human population as well.

"He's never mentioned you before," Stan said slowly.

Gwen crossed her arms under her chest, making sure to draw attention to her cleavage, and she pouted even more fiercely. "Does Chrispen know who all of *your* cousins are?"

"Well...no," Stan admitted, a blush heating his cheeks, "but I'm not a notorious—" He broke off, clamping his mouth shut. It was obvious he was afraid to accuse her 'cousin' of being exactly what he was, a violent thug. Which meant she'd been right, Mario and his buddy Chrispen weren't just making the supernatural community miserable. It seemed that Mario and his stooges didn't have a problem intimidating anyone, regardless of which society they belonged to.

Gwen was banking on the fact that most people knew it was better for their health to always give a Winthrow what they wanted. "Notorious what?" she asked a little haughtily.

Her indignant anger seemed to convince Stan that she was indeed part of the Winthrow clan. "Nothing!" he said quickly, his eyes full of fear. "I'm sorry, Miss Winthrow. I'll bring the car down for you right away."

Gwen's smile returned full force, though she was feeling slightly guilty for scaring the poor kid. "You're such a peach!" As Stan scurried away to fetch Chrispen's vehicle, she let her gaze flick across the street to where Hunter was waiting in her car. She quickly averted her eyes, not wanting to draw attention to him. She made a point to turn her back on Hunter's position, so she wouldn't even be tempted to glance his way. She shuffled her feet and tugged at her uncomfortable clothes. She desperately wanted out of this outfit. She felt ridiculous. It had probably been a good hundred years since she'd been in a dress. It wasn't like she dated. She had no use for such feminine things. This thought caused her to frown and glance across the street despite her attempts to avoid looking in that direction. She didn't date. Nor did she want to...right?

Luckily, Stan took that moment to return with Chrispen's car. He climbed out of the driver seat and held the keys out toward her. "Here you are, Miss Winthrow." His eyes were trained on the ground as if it was suddenly interesting.

Pretending she didn't notice the young man's fear, Gwen threw her arms around his neck and gave him a loud, smacking kiss on the cheek. "You're a total doll, the absolute best!" She plucked the keys from his fingers and flounced to the car before he could change his mind. Without a second look at the valet, she turned over the engine as if she'd been in this car a million times. Then she peeled away from the restaurant.

In her rearview mirror, Gwen saw Hunter pull out behind her. The hardest part was over. All that was left was for them to duplicate the key and get the car back before Chrispen decided he was ready to leave.

It was seven minutes to the nearest Wal-Mart, which was where they'd decided to have the key copied. Those seven minutes felt like an eternity. They were racing against the clock, and every minute that passed made her more and more anxious to get the car returned. If Chrispen caught them at this stage in the game, Marla was as good as dead. As she pulled into the lot, Gwen chose a parking space in the center in an attempt to hide the flashy car behind others.

Hunter pulled swiftly into the free space next to her, and they both climbed simultaneously out of their cars.

"I can't believe that worked," she admitted as Hunter strode over to her. "It was too easy. It-" She broke off with a startled gasp when Hunter grabbed her wrist and pulled her toward him. She was more than a little surprised when his lips pressed passionately to hers.

He chuckled deep in his throat, presumably at the surprised sound that escaped her at his actions. With one arm around her tiny waist, his other nudged one of her arms so that it slid around his neck.

Gwen was too startled to protest as he stepped closer, pressing her against his chest. She was tense for a moment, her eyes wide in surprise, but it didn't take long for her to relax against him. Both of her arms were somehow around his neck, and she couldn't remember for the life of her how the second one had gotten there. As she leaned into him, her lips softened against his, and her eyelashes fluttered closed. The kiss ended too quickly for her taste, but then she remembered that elves needed to come up for air. As their lips parted, she breathed, "What was that for?"

"For looking so damn amazing," Hunter said softly, his breath hot against her lips. "When you started pouting for that valet kid, I thought I was going to die of jealousy."

She tried not to grin at that and overcompensated with a

frown that looked suspiciously similar to a pout. She silently prayed she hadn't subconsciously just done that to get his attention.

At her pout, Hunter pulled her closer to him with a little groan. His mouth was on hers an instant later, soft and searching.

Gwen's arms slid down his neck until she gripped the front of his collar tightly in her fists. She clung to him, her lips parting slightly. Damn, he tasted good. Like...peppermint. She couldn't get enough of him.

Warning bells started going off in her mind. She couldn't let herself get distracted like this when lives were at stake, especially not by someone as infuriating as Hunter. Her arms slid down his chest, and she pushed. Her mouth wrenched away from his, and she staggered backwards. "We can't do this," she said breathlessly.

Hunter rubbed at his chest where she'd shoved him, his expression bewildered. "Can't do what, Gwen? Have feelings for each other?"

Gwen stalked toward the doors of the store, and Hunter was quick to follow, practically stepping on her heels. "We can't let ourselves get caught up in silly physical attraction," she reasoned. "There's a little girl's life on the line here. We both need to start acting like professionals instead of a couple of teenagers."

"What if it's not just physical attraction?"

He was rewarded with a less than dainty snort. "Think about what you're saying," Gwen instructed as she maneuvered through the store. "Honestly give it serious thought. You're an elf! I'm a vampire! Those two things don't mix. Ever." She strode purposely back to the area where the store copied keys. "Your body is telling you that you want something, but your brain should know better. Listen to your brain. As fun as a one night roll in the hay might be, we have responsibilities to concentrate on, so please keep our goal in mind."

Hunter watched as she slapped Chrispen's keys onto the counter in front of the worker. He wanted to shake her but figured it would draw unwanted attention to them.

"I want all of these copied," she demanded, purposefully keeping her gaze straight ahead.

Hunter gave a sigh at her business-like tone and leaned

against the counter as the man behind it bustled off to do as Gwen ordered. "Maybe I like you," he offered.

She shot him a derisive, skeptical look. "Because I've been so nice to you," she said sarcastically.

Hunter eyed her with mock thoughtfulness. "Perhaps you're right. Maybe it is just animal attraction." He turned sideways to face her, his elbow still resting on the counter. "You want to know the best way to get rid of temptation?"

Gwen raised her eyebrows in question. "What's that?"

"Give in to it," Hunter said, voice low and husky. He pushed off the counter and moved closer to her. "If you indulge yourself in temptation, it will no longer be so distracting." Standing so he could see her better, his hand went to the side of her neck, and his thumb caressed the hollow of her throat. "You'll be able to think much clearer if you get me out of your system."

Gwen stood frozen as he lowered his head to brush his lips against hers.

"It will feel so good," he drawled, pausing before saying, "to be able to think with a clear head."

Gwen's knees were quivering. She closed her eyes and shivered as Hunter grazed his lips along her jaw. She took a moment to collect herself before opening her eyes to stare at him. "Do you know an even better way to overcome temptation?"

He grinned slyly in response. "What's that?" he asked, his fingers skimming along her throat.

"Eliminate the temptation," she said darkly. Slapping his hand away, she narrowed her eyes. "I don't want to have to lock you inside your room when we get back home. Learn to control yourself so I won't have to."

Hunter took a step back, his hand dropping away from her. "You wouldn't lock me up like some kind of hostage," he argued, but his tone sounded surprised, as if he believed that she would do just that.

The worker took this moment to return with their keys. He set them on the counter between the two of them and looked expectantly for money as he gave the total.

Glad for the distraction, Gwen reached inside her purse for her wallet.

Seeing her reach for a credit card, Hunter stopped her and pulled out his own wallet. "Here. Let me."

Gwen narrowed her eyes at him, feeling more annoyed than grateful. "I don't need you to pay for this. I can handle it." Her expression turned even more hostile as she said, "Though I guess when you have a hundred thousand coming to you, ten dollars doesn't matter."

Hunter silently handed over a twenty dollar bill. His expression was one of anger, but he refused to comment. Once their purchase was complete and they had walked a few feet away with the keys safely in his pocket, he sent her an exasperated look. "Cash is untraceable."

"What?" she snapped irritably, not following where he was going with that statement.

"Cash is untraceable," he repeated. "If Chrispen somehow finds out someone copied his keys, and you paid with a credit card, there's a chance he'll be able to trace it back to you. It's a slim one, but why take any chances?"

Gwen stopped abruptly in her tracks, sending him a wounded look. "You don't get it, do you?"

Hunter stopped as well, alarmed by the tone of her voice. "Get what?" he asked warily. The almost fragile look on her face caused his heart to pick up speed. He didn't like it when the overconfident vampire didn't look as if she had everything under control.

Gwen sighed and shifted uneasily on her feet. "The cash idea was a nice gesture, but they're not going to need a credit card to trace this fiasco back to me."

"What are you talking about?" he asked, not liking where this conversation was going.

Gwen's expression was unhappy when she spoke. "Mario knew Dr. Wilson was my contact, because I busted a few of his goons with information supplied to me by Wilson. Kidnapping Marla was his way of throwing down a challenge. If we somehow manage to rescue Marla, they're going to know I was behind it."

She let out a troubled breath and began walking again, raking fingers through her hair. "If we get that girl out of their possession alive, they're going to come after me. I'm hoping to help the Wilsons' skip town before that happens. After that..." She shrugged. "Mario likes to strike fear into his enemies. A lot of times he likes to rape, mutilate, and torture his victims, then set them loose for others to learn from. I'm hoping he'll let me live, make an example out of me. It is going to be either a little girl or me. I'd rather have it be me."

Hunter stared at her in horror. "You can't be serious." He ran his hands through his shaggy brown hair as they exited the store and began weaving through the parking lot. The movement was one of uncertainty and fear, of helplessness. "You're just going to let them do this to you?"

Gwen shot him an agitated look, trying to keep the fear out of her eyes. "Of course I'm not going to just lie down and let them have me. I'll fight them as best as I can. The problem is, I'm going up against a very powerful group with a numbers advantage on their side. The odds aren't in my favor."

"Well, you have Colton-"

Gwen interrupted him. "I'd better not! Mario doesn't know of Colton's involvement, and he won't. There won't be any rape or torture for Colton. They'd murder him, and I don't want that on my hands. Colton had better stay out of this. It's better for everyone this way."

Hunter grabbed her arm in disbelief and spun her to face him. "I refuse to accept that answer. Together, we can fight them."

Gwen tried unsuccessfully to tug her arm free of his grasp. "Who's *we*? Don't tell me you suddenly care about something other than the money."

"I told you..." Hunter gave a growl of frustration. "I thought I made it quite clear that I care about more than just the money."

Gwen stared up at him, her blue eyes looking almost sad. "You can't save me. Stop trying. After we rescue the girl, you're going to take your money and go back to your life as if none of this ever happened." With that, she turned and walked away.

He watched her climb into Chrispen's car with fear evident in her posture. As she shut the door and started the car, Hunter whispered, "I'm going to do everything in my power to save you, Gwen, because it's too late for me to just walk away."

Chapter 6

Gwen stretched her arms above her head and let out a long yawn. She'd been tossing and turning for the last half hour. The sun wouldn't be down for at least another two hours, but she was too antsy to sleep.

Assuming Colton was still tucked away in bed, she padded barefoot and pajama clad toward the kitchen, her mind wrapped up in the events scheduled for later in the evening. Two days after copying Chrispen's key, they were finally going after Marla. The plan seemed solid, and the day matched up with a social event Mario was supposed to be attending. If all went well, he wouldn't even be home when they broke in.

Yawning again, Gwen bumped the swinging kitchen door open with her hip and ventured inside. The sight that greeted her almost made her jaw drop.

Hunter sat at the table with a bowl of cereal in front of him. In his hand was a carton of milk, frozen in the air, about to be poured into the bowl. At his elbow sat her box of Honey Nut Cheerios.

Gwen didn't know whether to laugh or be angry...or perhaps embarrassed. She hadn't thought that Hunter might be around. She'd been carefully avoiding him the past couple of days as best as possible. She couldn't stand the sad, pitying looks he kept giving her, so she'd kept her distance.

Now she was rooted to the floor in front of him wearing nothing but a tiny pair of boy shorts and a tank top. With no bra, no pants underneath, she stared at him in mortification; a blush deepening on her pale cheeks. She couldn't even find her voice to even complain about the Cheerios now that her mind was on her unclothed state.

It was Hunter who finally broke the silence. "I didn't expect you to be up so early." His eyes flicked to her breasts, but were quick to return to her face. Regardless of his swift correction, it looked as if it was taking a real effort to keep his gaze from straying to her half-exposed body.

Gwen wrapped her arms self-consciously around her waist. "I couldn't sleep," she said quietly.

Hunter suddenly had no trouble keeping his eyes on her face at the sound of anxiety in her voice. "Aw, Gwen," he said gently, guessing what had her so concerned, "you don't have to be afraid. I never had any intention of letting you fight this battle alone."

Never one for pity, Gwen began pacing the kitchen in agitation. "I'm not concerned about myself. I'm worried that we might be too late to help Marla. I'm worried about what they've already done to that poor little girl."

Hunter sat the milk down on the table and climbed to his feet. He walked to the middle of the room, putting himself on a collision course with her pacing.

When she whipped around, Gwen careened to a stop inches from crashing into him. "Get out of my way," she snarled.

Ignoring her demand, he grabbed her by the shoulders. "You don't have to take on everything alone. Not everything is your responsibility."

Gwen tried to yank away from him. "Someone's got to be responsible." She let out a frustrated huff when he wouldn't release her. Her eyes turned cold, and she hissed out her next sentence. "I don't need your help."

Hunter's grip tightened when she struggled. "No," he agreed. "You might not need my help, but isn't it nice to have someone else in your corner every once in awhile? I want to be there for you."

Gwen felt trapped. Her heart was pounding frantically in her chest, and it was suddenly harder to breathe. "I have Colton," she reminded him.

Hunter nodded. "You do." He set her with a serious look. "But you can keep him at an arm's length. It's not intimate." Hunter leaned closer, lowering his face over hers. "And I don't think he'd die for you."

His breath was hot on her face, and Gwen had a hard time concentrating on her argument. "I wouldn't want him to." The implication of his statement startled her as it sunk in. "Are you saying you would?"

One of Hunter's hands released her arm to gently graze along her cheek. "Possibly."

"Why?" she asked in surprise.

"I don't know," Hunter admitted honestly. "I can't stop the way I feel about you. I've tried. I just know that I can't let Mario's goons hurt you. As much as it terrifies me, I'd do anything to keep you safe."

"But I'm a vampire," she pointed out. "You're an elf."

"You think I haven't told myself that a hundred times?" he asked in annoyance. "It doesn't seem to matter."

"No," Gwen admitted softly. Seemingly with a will of their own, her fingers brushed along Hunter's abdomen. "It doesn't seem to matter." His hand grazed her cheek, and she leaned into his touch.

Taking this as encouragement, Hunter lowered his mouth that last little bit to kiss her. He was tentative at first, waiting to see if she would push him away.

She didn't. Gwen leaned into his chest, making a soft noise of enjoyment in the back of her throat. She was finally admitting to herself that she wanted Hunter. It didn't matter that he was an elf or that they came from two completely different worlds. There was something about him that she found unbelievably appealing.

At her unexpected responsiveness, Hunter gave a predatory growl. Both his hands slid down her backside, and he pulled her forcefully against himself.

Gwen gave a startled gasp into his mouth. "I thought you guys were supposed to be gentle creatures."

He chuckled wickedly, lowering his mouth to nibble along her jaw. "When have I ever fit your stereotypes?"

Gwen had to admit he had a point there. Everything about him broke the mold of what she expected from an elf. She slid her arms around his waist, clutching the fabric of his shirt. "You were right about you being in my system," she informed him. "There's only one way to stop thinking about you..."

Hunter's arms were suddenly lifting her off the ground. With a noise of desire, he wrapped her legs around his waist and sat her on the kitchen table. He half fell on top of her, using an arm to brace himself.

"I don't want you out of my system," Gwen said a moment before his mouth returned to hers.

He kissed her long and roughly. His free hand pressed against her back, holding her to him.

"I want you to overload my system," Gwen continued when Hunter finally came up for air.

"I'll overload your system alright," he promised. Finding his balance and no longer needing to brace himself, Hunter slid his hand up her stomach until he cupped her right breast in his hand.

Gwen whimpered into his mouth, arching up against his palm.

Hunter groaned. "You have no clue how badly I want you," he said, voice low and gravelly.

She pulled back only far enough to give herself the room to yank his shirt up. "Off," she demanded. Once he assisted her in getting the shirt over his head, she said, "I do have a clue. I've wanted you since the moment I first saw you bent over that car."

Hunter tossed his shirt behind him to the floor. "You could have had me then, right there in the garage."

She was back in his arms an instant later. Her mouth was on his, and her hands were splayed along his chest. The thought of having sex in a dirty, greasy garage was somehow a turn on. Grabbing his belt buckle, she yanked him closer.

At the sudden movement, Hunter reached out to catch himself. His hand hit the carton of milk. It toppled over and poured along the table, dripping to the floor. "Shit," he said with a chuckle.

Gwen shifted to avoid the dribbling milk, laughing at the mess they'd created. Wrapping an arm around his neck, she pulled him down for a slow, sensual kiss. She didn't argue as his hands ventured up her shirt. She took the opportunity to unfasten his belt with her free hand.

At that moment, the kitchen door swung open and Colton's girlfriend Penelope walked in. Her eyes widened at the sight of the couple sprawled across the table.

Gwen frantically batted at Hunter's chest in an attempt to squirm out from under him. "You need to be more careful!

You spilled milk everywhere." She ran her fingers quickly through her sleep-tousled hair, attempting to look presentable. "It's a good thing we got your shirt off before all this milk had a chance to get all over you and leave a stain." She cringed at her own statement. She didn't think milk stained, but it was the first thing that came to mind.

Penelope raised an eyebrow at the obvious lie, an amused smirk on her lips. "Don't mind me. I'm just taking my prenatal vitamin."

That statement startled Gwen. Colton was a vampire. He couldn't have children. Surely Penny knew that.

Before she could comment, Hunter beat her with a statement nearly as shocking. "Colton's girlfriend is an elf?" he asked in incredulity.

Gwen's head whipped in his direction so fast she nearly fell over. "What?" She spun to face Penelope. "Penny is not an elf."

"Half elf actually," Penny offered. "Dad was an elf. My mother was a pixie."

Gwen sucked in a deep breath of disbelief. She braced her hand against the table, not even noticing that her fingers were in the milk. "I...I didn't know. You never said anything..." She was suddenly remembering every nasty elf comment she'd made in front of Penny, all the things she'd said to Colton when his girlfriend... "I am so sorry."

Penny shrugged. "You didn't mean anything personal by it. At least not to me personally." She gave Gwen an understanding smile. "All those times when you were saying something bad about elves, you didn't even know I was one. It was almost comical in a way. I was never offended by it."

Gwen let out a relieved sigh that Penny once again proved she had the personality of a saint. Once able to think past relief, she stared at Penny, really stared at her.

Penelope's hair was a pretty, golden blond that hung nearly to her elbows. She was tall and willowy, almost fragile looking. Her eyes were a sparkling green a few shades lighter than Hunter's. They were elf eyes.

Before Gwen could think of something to say, Penny smiled again. "I'm heading back to bed. Continue as if I'd never been here." She winked at Hunter on her way out.

He smirked devilishly in return. "See ya, sweetie."

Gwen blinked in surprise at the open friendliness between

the two of them. It was like they were both mocking her in some way, acting as if she was naive. She supposed she deserved it. She'd been making fun of their race since as long as she could remember. She pressed a hand to her forehead. "I feel so terrible."

Hunter moved to stand in front of her. His hands gripped her hips, and he stepped in closer to pin her against the table. "Fooling around with me helps your reputation." He lifted her hand out of the spilled milk. He watched as a drop formed on her fingertip. He brought the hand to his mouth and sucked the milk from her finger, his tongue sliding sensually along her skin. "It proves you can't hate us too much." Loosening his grip on her hand, he kissed her fingertips. "You're working on improving your vampire/elf relations."

Releasing her hand, he placed two fingers under her chin and tilted her face up to him. Lowering his mouth, he kissed her gently. "Don't feel pressured to fall into this immediately. Just take baby steps." He grinned. "Let's try something easy." He brushed her hair away from her face. "Like breakfast. You want to have a bowl of Honey Nut Cheerios with me?"

Gwen couldn't help but grin. "You are determined to get your hands on my Cheerios."

"That's not all I'm determined to get my hands on," Hunter said, voice full of seduction.

"Let's just start with cereal," Gwen said nervously.

Hunter seemed to accept this answer. "I'm happy with that." Cupping her face in his hands, he kissed her forehead. "Take a seat. I'll clean up this mess and get us some breakfast."

Gwen sunk into a chair at the kitchen table. She watched as Hunter moved around her kitchen, appearing perfectly at ease. She liked the way he looked as he opened cabinets and rifled through a drawer to get her a spoon. He looked like he belonged here, and the fact that she enjoyed that scared her. Could she actually be falling for Hunter, for an elf?

Chapter 7

Gwen stared up at the dark and silent home of Mario Cessarini. Her stomach tightened with anxiety at the thought that she might die in that house, that Marla may have already died there.

Hunter's hand was suddenly pressed against her lower back. "We're going to get her out, Gwen. I promise."

She nodded, too nervous to speak.

Hunter moved past her, his hand sliding away. He walked up to the gate at the entrance. Pulling their set of copied keys from his pocket, he flipped through them, looking for the one most likely to fit into the gate. "Colton better be right about you being sneaky, my little Gwen doll. It would be best if we could get the girl out before having to worry about retaliation. It will be easier to keep you safe when we don't have a child to protect and we're on our own territory."

As he chose a key and slid it into the lock of the gate, Gwen grimaced. She didn't want to fight these men on her own territory. She didn't want to risk putting Colton in danger...or Hunter. She shuddered at the thought of what Mario's people would do to an elf.

Mistaking her reaction as fear for herself, Hunter put a comforting hand against her back. "Don't worry, Gwenny. I promise to keep you safe. I'll protect you with my life." With that, he inched open the gate and edged inside.

"That's what I'm afraid of," Gwen whispered into the dark night. With a soft sigh, she followed him through the gate.

Without needing to be asked, she kept an eye on their

surroundings while Hunter relocked the gate behind them. Nothing stirred, and she didn't hear any alarms going off. Maybe Hunter's plan would work. She prayed that they'd be able to get Wilson's family out of town before anyone realized Marla was missing.

"There's a side door," Hunter whispered in her ear. "There's no security camera there. It's Mario and Chrispen's private entry." He started in the direction of the secret entrance, sticking to the shadows as best as he could. He avoided the glare of the floodlights, his eyes ever watchful for cameras and guards.

Gwen followed after him, blending in fluidly with the darkness. She moved in silence, easily keeping pace with him. "No camera. Sounds promising," she said softly.

Hunter snorted. "They figure no one's dumb enough to try to break in through that door. The security system automatically changes the password every three minutes. There are only two electronic devices that are sent the current code. Mario has one, Chrispen the other. It's nearly impossible to get through this door. You get that code wrong once, and they light this place up. Alarms, searchlights, dogs, you name it. You mess up once, and they lock the entire place down. It's too damn risky to go through that door, and everyone knows it."

"Then why are we going through it?" Gwen squeaked, not liking the sound of that.

"Remember those skills you hired me for?" Hunter asked with a crooked grin. "This is where that comes in."

As they reached the door, Gwen bit her lip in anxiety. "You're that good?" she asked. "Good enough to do the impossible?"

Taking a deep breath, Hunter placed his hand over the small box that held the keypad. "We're about to find out. I've never used magic this way, but in theory, it should work." His eyes closed in concentration.

Gwen gaped at him in disbelief. "In theory?" she cried. "We're breaking in here on a theory?" She felt her heart pounding a panicked rhythm in her chest, not an easy feat for a vampire. "Why aren't we just doing what you did the last time? Obviously, that worked. This," she said, waving at the door, "is untested."

Hunter opened his eyes to stare at her. "You don't want

to go in the way I did last time. Trust me."

Her stomach plummeted, sinking to her toes. "How did you get in last time?" she whispered, fearing she wasn't going to like his answer.

"I went in through the front door," Hunter said, his eyes locked on hers. "I drove a car through the front gate, kicked the front door down, and stormed in with a shotgun full of silver bullets."

Gwen felt as if she'd been punched in the gut. His last approach had been anything but stealthy. "How...why?" she asked, bracing an arm against the building.

"I wasn't looking to sneak off anonymously after I was done. I was looking for revenge." He sighed, eyes remorseful. "One of Mario's thugs tried to rape my sister. He beat the living hell out of her." His eyes blazed with anger. "You talked about the stereotypical, breakable elf, Gwen? That's my sister. She's like this fragile little china doll, and he broke her. Do you know what it's like to watch someone you love bleed and cry and fear for their life?" He shook his head, a cruel glint in his normally friendly eyes. "I didn't care what happened to me. I just wanted that man dead. I may be known for my stealth skills, but this isn't one of the instances where I used them. So I'd recommend we do things differently this time. I think caution is a little higher on my list."

Gwen's hand was covering her mouth, and her eyes were wide in horror. "Wh...what happened...last time?" she asked, her sentence sounding disjointed.

"I killed him," Hunter said evenly. His eyes slid back to the keypad. "Turns out he was forcing himself on Mario's sister as well. My invasion of privacy gave her the courage to speak up. Mario thanked me for helping to avenge what was done to his sister. Then he warned me if he ever caught me near his house again, he'd blow my head off. Apparently rape is only okay as long as it doesn't affect him personally."

Gwen gaped, a chill running down her arms. "Then why are you here?" she asked, her voice shrill with alarm. She grabbed his wrist, giving it a frantic tug. "We have to get you out of here. It was insane for you to come here! You're lucky you got to live the first time. If he catches you here again, he won't just kill you, he'll torture you to death. Why would you ever come back?"

He turned to her, a soft smile on his lips. "Why does a

man ever do anything stupid? Because of a girl." He tucked a stray piece of hair behind her ear. "I unwisely let myself fall head over heels for this vampire chick. She's a real pain in the ass too. It takes a real fool to risk his life for a woman who's afraid of commitment and doesn't even like elves, but when was I ever smart?"

"Hunter," Gwen said softly, her heart pounding for a different reason now. "This is crazy. They'll kill you."

"Sure it's crazy," he said with a casual shrug, "but what have you got to lose?"

"You," she said softly.

Hunter suddenly began punching numbers into the keypad. A light flashed green, and the locks slid back. He tossed her a mischievous grin. "It's a good thing you don't like me very much then." With that, he cracked the door and slipped inside.

Cursing under her breath at his inability to be serious even in a time like this, Gwen followed after Hunter. She followed him down darkened hallways, through corridors that all looked alike to her, and past closed doors. The place seemed more like an office building than a home. She wasn't sure how Hunter knew where he was going, but he seemed to be moving through the building with intent.

Twice she went to beg him to turn back. Twice she reached for his hand to stop him from continuing but chickened out. She was too afraid to tell him how she felt about him, to let him know he was too important to lose.

It seemed as if Hunter sensed her uncertainty. As he stopped in front of a door, he grabbed her hand and pulled her toward him. He held her hand tightly in his, seemingly unconscious of his actions. He nodded to the locked door in front of them. "She's in there."

Gwen stepped in close to him, her voice lowered to an almost inaudible whisper. "How can you be sure?" she breathed, glancing nervously over her shoulder at the hallway behind them.

Hunter grimaced. "Whoever is in this room is radiating terror. I can feel it." On her confused look, he explained. "Elf skills. We're very attuned to emotions." He paused, his attention returning to the door. "Unless they've got more than one prisoner they're holding hostage, Marla is behind this door." A frightened look spread across his face. "God I hope they don't make a habit of keeping hostages."

"No, they don't," Gwen said. "At least not for long."

Hunter's expression turned sympathetic. "It's not going to be you behind one of these doors." He lowered his head and kissed her briefly. "I won't let that happen."

She stared up at him, unsure of what to say. She desperately wanted to believe him, to let him protect her. It would feel nice to have someone take care of her just this once, to care about what happened to her. She opened her mouth to say as much then froze, her ears straining. "Someone's coming."

She stepped back, her eyes staring intently down the darkened hallway. "I'll take care of whoever it is. You just worry about getting that door open." Before Hunter could argue, she melded into the darkness. She moved silently down the hallway until she found a corner dark enough where she could be hidden when pressed against the wall.

A moment later, a man came walking around the corner. Gwen pegged him immediately as a werewolf. He was beefed up, muscles rippling from arms that were too big to be natural. His neck was thicker than one of her thighs. She rolled her eyes at that. Werewolves. Some of them, these henchmen types, were nothing more than dumb dogs on steroids.

The werewolf in question was strolling along, whistling under his breath. To him, this had to seem like a cake job. No one was dumb enough to try to break into Mario Cessarini's home. This place was like a fortress. Besides, if someone were stupid enough to try a break-in, they'd get caught way before this point in the building. He probably thought his job was nothing more than to please Mario's paranoid mind. He was wrong.

Gwen let him walk past her.

Werewolves had an excellent sense of smell, but vampires were nearly impossible to detect. Elves on the other hand...

Gwen waited. She let him pick up Hunter's scent, that earthy, fresh rain smell. She felt a zip of adrenaline at the mere memory of his intoxicating scent. She quickly returned her attention to the werewolf in front of her.

He'd tensed, and a low growl rumbled from his throat.

Hunter was just barely visible in the dim lighting if you were looking for him. His scent though was like a flashing light.

The werewolf took an aggressive step forward. "What the hell do you think you're doing?" he demanded.

Hunter spun to face him, eyes wide.

When the werewolf's attention was fully on Hunter, Gwen attacked. He was taller than she was by a good foot. She needed his neck, which meant she needed him on his knees.

Creeping up behind the werewolf that probably outweighed her by two hundred pounds, Gwen delivered a vicious kick to the back of one of his knees. It buckled. As soon as he collapsed to the carpet, her arms were around his neck, choking back his supply of oxygen.

Hunter's green eyes widened even further at the sight of her overpowering the struggling werewolf. He took a tentative step in her direction, and then paused uncertainly.

"Get the door open!" she snapped, breath labored from the struggle.

Hunter hesitated only a moment before turning back to the key coded lock.

She was relieved for that. She wasn't worried about winning this fight. She'd jumped the poor guy. He didn't even stand a chance, especially when he wasn't even in wolf form. She was more worried about how unflattering and less than dainty this situation must make her appear. She was half on top of the werewolf's back, unable to get any further onto him due to his bulk. Her face was red with exertion, and she could just imagine the vein in her forehead popping out in an unfavorable manner.

She gave a rough jerk on the werewolf's neck, trying to stop his struggling. She tightened her grip as his body began to go slack, making certain he wouldn't be getting back up for a while. She couldn't feel all that bad about choking him. He worked for a mobster, and he'd growled at her elf.

Gwen blinked in surprise at that thought as she dropped the unconscious werewolf to the floor. Her elf? When had Hunter made the transition into *her* elf? She didn't even like elves.

She was still pondering that when Hunter said, "I'm in."

She quickly pushed her concerns involving him to the back of her mind and rushed to his side. "Is she in there? Is she in there?"

Hunter slid her a sideways look, raising an eyebrow. "Can

I get the door open? I'll have a better assessment of the situation then."

She shot him an annoyed glare, but stepped back, giving him room.

He eased the door open, though it still made an audible click as the latch came free. Inside was a dimly lit room. Both of them peered inside, their breath held in anticipation.

"Marla?" Gwen asked quietly. She glanced nervously at Hunter before tiptoeing into the darkness.

Huddled in the far corner against the wall was a small girl with red hair.

Gwen rushed toward her, and the girl let out a terrified cry.

The tiny redhead held out a hand to motion Gwen to stay back. "Leave me alone," she cried, her voice edging on hysterical.

Gwen screeched to a halt, her boots squeaking on the tile floor. "Marla," she whispered soothingly, "we're here to help you. I'm a friend of your father. He's really worried about you." She took a tentative step forward. "We're going to take you home, but I need you to be very, very quiet so the bad guys don't hear us, okay?"

Marla began sobbing soft tears of relief at Gwen's words. She bobbed her head, wiping at her tears. "Okay," she whispered.

Gwen nodded her pleasure at the girl's bravery, though her lips were a grim line. "Can you walk?"

"Yeah," Marla said, her voice trembling. Though her words were shaky, her expression was determined. She climbed slowly to her feet, taking hesitant steps out of her cold, dark corner.

Gwen tried to give her a reassuring smile, but it came off as tense. She turned and pointed at Hunter who was still hovering in the doorway, sending nervous glances down the hall. "This is my friend Hunter. He's one of the good guys. You can trust him."

Hunter glanced up and flashed Gwen a quick, affectionate smile.

She couldn't help but return his smile, but her gaze was quick to return to Marla. "I want you to stick with Hunter. He'll keep you safe. Whatever happens, stay with him."

"Okay," Marla promised.

Not wanting to waste anymore time, Gwen marched purposefully back to the door. She didn't look behind her as she pushed into the hallway. She trusted that Hunter would follow. She continued past the body of the downed werewolf, not even giving it a second glance.

It was Marla who gave a frightened little gasp as she inched past the hulking form of the werewolf. Though he was in human form, the sight of him still caused the little girl to tremble in fear. An instant later, her eyes hardened. "Big bully," she accused the unconscious man under her breath.

Gwen moved on, retracing their steps, making a hasty retreat from the cramped prison.

Hunter didn't even dare breathe for fear of attracting attention until they were safely back in the car, speeding toward the highway.

The drive to Marla's home was short. None of them spoke while Gwen put more and more distance between them and Mario's thugs.

When she finally put the car in park a mile from Marla's home, Gwen finally began to relax a little. She spun in her seat to face the girl, her eyes appraising. "How badly are you hurt?"

Marla winced and shifted in her seat. "I'm not too bad. I think my arm's broken though."

"Her arm is definitely broken," Hunter mumbled from beside Marla in the backseat.

Gwen sighed. "I was afraid of that. I was hoping we could get your family out of town before anyone realized you'd gone missing. Unfortunately, we should probably stop by the hospital to get that arm looked at."

Hunter sent Gwen a sly grin. "Actually, we don't have to go to the hospital. I can fix her up right here."

"You're going to fix a broken arm?" Gwen asked skeptically. "You have a cast tucked into your pants somewhere?"

Hunter tossed her a sexy, crooked smile. "I'm an elf, Gwenny. Besides being vampire food, this is what we're good at." He turned in his seat to face Marla. "Okay. This is going to hurt. I apologize in advance."

Gwen watched in curiosity as Hunter delicately felt along Marla's broken arm.

His face was scrunched in concentration as he slid his long fingers across her pale arm. He paused when he came to the point where the bone appeared to be broken, though

Gwen had no clue how he could tell for sure that he was at the precise spot. "Hold your breath," he advised.

Marla did as instructed, her eyes wide in anticipation of the pain.

Hunter gripped her arm tightly in both hands and yanked.

There was an audible pop, and Marla's breath came out in a squeak of pain.

"I'm sorry," Hunter rushed out, "very, very sorry, but that's the worst of it. I promise."

Marla clenched her teeth and stayed silent.

Hunter gripped the girl's arm between his hands, and his brow furrowed in concentration.

Before Gwen's eyes, Marla's skin began to glow softly. Her eyes flicked to Hunter's face in astonishment. "Are you..." She stopped, barely believing it. "Are you healing her?" she finally asked.

Hunter bobbed his head, his long brown hair falling into his eyes. "Yes." He smiled softly, his hands still gliding gently along Marla's arm. "Remember in your kitchen this morning when Penny said she was taking her prenatal vitamins?"

"Yes," Gwen said, voice suspicious.

"All elves have minor healing abilities. Penny can..." His expression became sheepish, almost embarrassed. "Penny can temporarily heal Colton's reproductive system, at least enough for them to possibly have a child."

"Vampires can't have children," Gwen protested, shaking her head in denial.

"They can," Hunter corrected. "It's just so rare because you guys are so hostile toward us. You don't care to find out how we can assist you. What Penny is doing isn't too compli-cated. You only need a male vampire's reproductive system in working order for a few hours. A female vampire on the other hand..." He shook his head, an amused smirk on his lips. "A female would need to be around a decent healer for her entire pregnancy."

Stunned by this information, Gwen watched in silent amazement as Hunter's fingertips slid gently along Marla's eyelid.

The girl's eye was puffy and bruised, but at Hunter's touch, her skin glowed, and the bruise began to disappear.

"You seem very good at that," Gwen observed.

"Better than most," Hunter admitted. "Most elves can

heal minor injuries. I can mend broken bones and torn muscle. My healing abilities transferred over into electronics. Why do you think I'm such a damn good mechanic?"

"You heal machines?" Gwen asked incredulously.

"Something like that," Hunter replied with a wicked grin. "All I need to do is place my hand on something, and I can sense what is broken or what's about to break." He shrugged as if this was no big deal. "That's how I can break into places so easily. I touch security boxes, and they will tell me codes, passwords, whatever it is I need." His gaze suddenly lowered to Marla, and he changed the subject. "Well, it looks like you're all healed. How do you feel?"

"Perfect!" Marla said in surprise. "That was awesome!"

Sensing that their conversation was over, Gwen started up the car, driving the last mile to Marla's house while the girl chatted happily to Hunter.

When they reached the house, the car was barely in park before Jared came rushing out.

Marla gave a cry of delight. She threw the car door open and lunged out, running to her awaiting father.

While the two embraced, Gwen and Hunter got out of the car and approached them with a more subdued pace.

Gwen stared at the father and daughter as they hugged. You would never guess the girl had been battered and broken not five minutes before. "You're quite talented," she said softly to the elf next to her.

Hunter smiled, crossing his arms proudly over his chest. "It's about time you started thinking of me as something besides a meal."

Gwen stood in silence, glancing occasionally at his tall, lanky frame. Before she could think of a response to his statement, Colton stepped from the house.

He nodded in their direction, a pleased look on his face.

"Looks like we're free to go," Gwen observed. "Colton is going to get them out of town. I was instructed that once the job was finished, I was to take you back to your home. You're no longer our prisoner." She glanced away, not wanting to look him in the eye. "Enjoy your freedom. You can come to our building tomorrow night to get your cat and your payment." Without another word, she turned and walked back to the car.

Chapter 8

The car ride to Hunter's apartment had been in awkward silence.

Gwen didn't want to talk about the fact that they would be parting ways, perhaps permanently. They'd only known each other a few days, so there was no reason to believe they'd have any further contact after Colton gave Hunter his money, but damn it, she liked him. Forcing that thought to the back of her mind, she threw the car into park in front of Hunter's place. "This is your stop," she said neutrally.

"It is," Hunter agreed. He sat in silence, staring out the windshield. After a few moments of silence, he let out a huffy sigh. "Why don't you come inside for a minute? I can heal you really fast."

Gwen turned to face him in surprise. "Heal what? I'm perfectly fine."

Hunter pointed to a deep looking scratch under the side of her upper arm. "That cut looks pretty bad."

Gwen glanced at it, noticing the blood on her shirt for the first time. "Damn werewolf," she cursed. "I didn't even notice he'd shifted his hands into claws."

"Obviously he did though," Hunter pointed out unnecessarily. He opened his door and climbed out. "Come inside. I'll have that arm good as new in no time."

Gwen hesitated only a moment before following him up the steps to his apartment. "I suppose there's no harm in letting you take a look at it."

Hunter pulled his key from his back pocket and opened

the door. He guided Gwen into the living room and motioned for her to take a seat on the couch.

Gwen sunk to the worn cushions, and Hunter sat next to her an instant later.

As gentle as he could be, Hunter's hands traveled along her injured arm.

Gwen watched in fascination as her skin began to tingle and glow. The torn flesh began to meld itself back together. In seconds, a wound that would have taken a vampire at least a few hours to heal was completely gone. She stretched out her arm, testing Hunter's healing job. "Impressive," she admitted.

"Thanks," Hunter said quietly, sounding almost bashful.

The silence between them returned. Gwen sat with her hands folded in her lap, wracking her brain for something, anything to say. When the silence seemed to stretch for too long, she pushed to her feet. "I should be going. Colton is supposed to call my cell phone to let me know when they get safely out of town, and I left it at home. I didn't want to have to worry about it ringing while we were in Mario's place."

Hunter was quick to follow her. "Let me walk you to the door."

Gwen walked self-consciously, her arms unmoving at her sides. When she reached the door, she said with a voice as stiff as her body, "Again, thank you for healing my arm."

"You're welcome," was his soft reply.

Gwen gripped the doorknob in her hand and twisted, opening the door slightly.

Fearful of her walking out of his life for good, Hunter said almost desperately, "Gwen, wait!" His words were rushed and breathless.

She turned toward him, her hand still on the doorknob. She tilted her head back to stare up into his face but didn't speak.

Hunter cupped her cheek in his hand. "Don't go," he requested in a low voice as he lowered his face over hers.

Gwen's hand slid off the doorknob the instant his mouth closed over hers. Her arms wound around his waist, and she stepped in against his warm chest.

Hunter's other hand reached out to the door. He pressed his palm flat against it, closing them in.

His hand slid to the back of her neck, and he tilted her

head back with his thumb against her jaw. His mouth was soft and searching, more tentative than anything else. "Stay with me," he whispered.

Gwen responded fiercely. She slid her arms up and around his neck, clinging to him. "Okay." She stood on her tiptoes so she could crush her lips to his. "I'm ready to give in to that temptation now."

Hunter smiled against her lips. "Should we..." He trailed off, his mouth drawn to hers again. It was like he couldn't stop kissing her.

Gwen nodded frantically, knowing what he was trying to ask. "Bedroom," she agreed.

Hunter's arms wrapped firmly around her waist. He spun her so her back was to the room, and he began walking her backwards through his apartment.

Laughing at his sudden eagerness, Gwen kicked her shoes off, leaving them in the hallway.

Following her lead, Hunter kicked off his shoes as well, laughing as one banged off the wall. His mouth never left hers as they reached his room, and he fumbled with the doorknob. Without looking, he managed to get the door to swing inward. Walking her inside, his hand automatically reached for the light switch.

Gwen's hand shot out to cover his. "No," she whispered. "We don't need it for what we're about to do."

Hunter groaned, his hand sliding away from the light switch. He realized she was right. He could dimly see her in the moonlight coming in through the window. They didn't need more light than that.

Impatiently, Gwen kicked the door shut. Gripping the front of his shirt in her fists, she pulled him over to the large bed. Placing a hand in the center of his chest, she pushed him to sit on the edge of the mattress. Her hands buried in his hair, running through the dark, silky locks. "I've never wanted this more in my life," she breathed, her mouth inches from his.

"Wow. That makes me feel good, because I bet you're pretty old."

Gwen's fingers tightened in his hair, and she pulled his head back so he stared into her eyes. "It's not very nice to call a girl old even if she *is* a vampire."

Hunter grinned the grin that made it impossible to stay

mad at him. "Here," he said, pulling her down to straddle him, "let me make it up to you." His mouth sought out her neck, nibbling softly along her jaw.

"Keep in mind you have a whole lot of making up to do," Gwen said with a pout, remembering his reaction the last time she'd protruded her bottom lip.

His reaction this time did not disappoint. Hunter growled low in his throat and gripped her hips tightly. "I'll do as much making up as you wish," he said. "I'll make it up to you as long as you want me too." His statement came off as sexual, promising that his idea of making things up to her would require both of them to be naked.

"Mmm," Gwen mumbled into his mouth, running her hands along his chest. "I think I'm going to want you to make it up to me for at least a few hours, minimum. I'll need you in less clothing though for the kind of attention I'm expecting. Much less." Her fingers reached out to grab the buttons on his shirt. She nimbly undid them and then began yanking at the sleeves in an attempt to get the shirt off. When they didn't yield to her demands immediately, she tugged harder. She was prepared to shred the fabric if need be, whatever it took to get him naked. She tugged again, putting even more force behind it. There was an audible 'pop', and Gwen froze with a gasp. "What was that?"

Hunter winced, and the corners of his eyes tightened. "Don't freak out," he warned.

"When you say it like that, how am I supposed to *not* freak?" Gwen asked with a squeak of fear. She tried to keep her heart from jumping out of her chest. "Hunter," she said, voice cautiously even, "what was that noise?"

Hunter's hands slid away from her hips, and he grabbed his left shoulder. "I think you dislocated my shoulder."

"What?" Gwen cried in horror, jumping away from him.

"I think you just-"

"I know what you said. I just...how...shit!" Gwen ran her fingers through her hair, feeling close to panicking. "This is what I meant when I said you guys break too easily! Oh my God, I broke you! I broke you by trying to have sex with you."

Hunter put a finger to her lips. "Gwen doll, chill." His hand returned to his shoulder. "We may break easier than you, but you forget how easily we heal." He yanked roughly, and his arm popped back into the socket. "See?" He ran his fingertips along his shoulder, and it began to glow softly.

Gwen reached out and brushed her fingers along his. Her own fingertips began to glow where she touched him. "Amazing," she whispered, feeling his magic tingle along her skin.

"It is," Hunter agreed, though he sounded as if he was talking about something other than his healing talents. He suddenly grabbed her face in his hands and kissed her vigorously. "Enough talking about my healing ability," he admonished. "If you don't get your sexy ass out of your clothes right this instant..."

Smiling, Gwen shifted on his lap, sliding closer to him. "If I don't take my clothes off, what?" she asked, leaning down to nip at his nose. She was still concerned about his arm, but when he was threatening to get her naked, he couldn't be hurt too badly. "What do you plan to do?"

With a low, manly chuckle, Hunter grabbed her waist and flipped her to lay on her back. "I'll turn my magic on you," he reasoned.

All worry about his arm flew from her mind. No way could he flip her so easily if he was still in any pain. Gwen wiggled underneath of him, rubbing her body against his. "You wouldn't," she challenged.

A wicked grin spread across his lips. "Oh wouldn't I?" he slid his hand slowly up the inside of her thigh.

Gwen felt a tingling burst of magic through her jeans. She gave a soft yip and bucked off the bed. "Holy crap!" she cried, surprised by the erotic feel of magic that was all Hunter as it teased along her skin.

Hunter chuckled and moved his hand to her waist. He gave her another soft burst of magic before sliding his hand up her shirt. "Have I made my point?" he asked with a crooked grin.

"You've made me realize how much I absolutely love elf magic," she offered. She wrapped her legs around his waist, holding him to her. "You've also convinced me to get naked if your magic feels that good through clothing. I can't wait to find out how you feel skin to skin."

"Funny," Hunter said in amusement. "I was just thinking the exact same thing about you." His hand was on her bare belly underneath her shirt. He gave her another jolt of energy. He then sat back on his knees and began shrugging out of his shirt, leaving himself in the tank he had underneath. "I think I'll handle this myself this time," he teased playfully.

Gwen frowned, and he chuckled, leaning in to give her a quick kiss. "Don't you dare look unhappy." He kissed her again, this time his lips lingering on hers a little longer. "I only want to see happy *'I'm having sex'* expressions on your face." His lips grazed along her jaw before he pulled back to stare at her. "Let's see it. I want to see happy face."

"You want to see happy face on a vampire?" Gwen asked, unable to keep herself from laughing.

Hunter ran his thumb along her bottom lip. "There it is, that pretty, fang-filled smile."

Gwen made a noise of mock annoyance and slapped his arm. "My fangs are retracted, you goof."

Hunter chuckled, giving her a lazy, casual kiss. "It's necessary for me to be goofy. Someone's got to balance out your moody vampire habits. It's the yin and yang of life, baby." Before Gwen could choose to be offended, he hopped up from the bed and stared down at her. His expression was thoughtful.

Gwen self-consciously wrapped an arm around her waist. "What..." She trailed off, her voice nervous. She wasn't used to men staring at her like this. When she chose to have sex, which wasn't often, she was more of a get in, get out type of girl. She didn't do foreplay well.

Hunter's lips curved into a grin at her uncertainty, and he reached down to grab her hands. He pulled her to her feet and stood her in front of him. "I just didn't want to pass up the opportunity of getting a full look at your beauty."

Gwen snorted and rolled her eyes. "Yeah. Okay."

Hunter's eyes widened in shock at her sarcastic tone. "You really don't think you're attractive." He shook his head disapprovingly. "You think you're just some mean, tough, ass -kicking creature of the night."

Gwen arched an eyebrow in response, confirming his theory.

With a sigh, Hunter closed the small distance between them. His hands slid up her neck, gently along the base of her head, and then ran through her hair. "First off," he said, leaning in to kiss the tip of her nose, "you have these gorgeous tresses."

Gwen quirked an eyebrow. "Are you sure you aren't gay? I offer you sex, and you'd rather rave about my hair."

Irritation flashed in his eyes, and with his hands still buried in her hair, he lowered his mouth to hers. He kissed her roughly, his lips hard and demanding. He forced her lips apart, and his tongue delved into her mouth. He plundered and explored, claiming her in a way so pushy, it sent a chill down her spine.

Gwen was suddenly glad she didn't need to breathe, because Hunter left her mind unable to function. She forgot about everything except him. Normally, she reminded herself to pull air through her lungs even though they no longer needed it. She played human, kept a low profile. Besides that, she still liked the feel of air, even if it wasn't crucial to her survival anymore. It made her feel fresh inside, alive. It let her forget what she truly was, a walking corpse. Now, all pretenses fell away. She forgot to inhale. Hell, she nearly forgot her own name. Had air been necessary, she would have toppled over.

Her temperature rose at the heated feel of Hunter's body as it pressed aggressively to hers. She responded to him fiercely. Her nails dug into the undershirt he was wearing under his button-up. After a moment, she noted with dissatisfaction that his kisses were getting gentler and gentler.

Then suddenly, Hunter's mouth left hers. "I'm positive I'm not gay," he informed her. "The things I want to do to you..." He brought his head down and flicked his tongue along her bottom lip before taking a step back. "Let's just say my thoughts need an adult rating."

He grinned at her with his lopsided smile for a moment before saying, "Now back to my ogling." Reaching out, he began undoing the buttons of her blouse. It was black, but he couldn't help noticing that it was soft and girly. "What's a vampire doing wearing a blouse anyway?"

He lowered his mouth to kiss a path down her throat, his fingers deftly continuing with the buttons of her blouse. He slid his lips across her collarbone, nipping playfully at the skin. When he got her shirt unbuttoned all the way, he slid it from her shoulders, his mouth never leaving her throat.

Gwen tilted her head back, enraptured by his caressing lips and slightly amused at his nibbling. She was a vampire. She was the one used to biting people, not the other way around. For the first time in forever, she let herself go. She simply relaxed and took pleasure in his attention. So what if he was an elf? He was her elf, and he was soft and warm. Her breath hitched as his fingers began fumbling with the button of her faded, torn jeans.

"There is something unbelievably sexy about a vampire in hip-huggers," Hunter breathed. His hands began forcing her pants over her hips, and he let them drop to the floor. "Though I'm betting you're even sexier out of them."

As her pants pooled at her ankles, Gwen lifted her feet to step out of them. She was left in her bra, a pair of ankle socks, and her panties.

With a little growl of approval, Hunter pulled her to him. He ran his hands along the creamy skin of her waist, nuzzling against her neck. When he was finally able to collect himself, he took a step back to stare at her. His eyes roved approvingly along her skin. "I thought I'd never get you out of your clothes. Though it wasn't due to lack of trying."

Gwen stood frozen as he circled her. She'd never been scrutinized so closely in her life. During sex in the past, she'd made sure it was unbelievably dark, and she'd undressed as quickly as possible before jumping under the covers. She'd never awarded a man the opportunity to stare at her like this. Hell, only two people had ever stared at her in her undergarments before, and one of them was dead. That list included her mother in the days when Gwen had been human, a few lifetimes ago. The only other person on that list was Colton, and that was because he didn't seem to value the sacred agreement between roommates that included knocking before entering bathrooms or bedrooms. She forgot all about her self-consciousness though when Hunter stepped into her.

He pressed himself against her back, his chest grazing along the clasp of her bra. His mouth lowered to her neck, and he kissed a trail up her throat. He reached her jaw and nuzzled against it. "You exceed my every expectation," he whispered in her ear.

Gwen shivered, both from the feel of his mouth and the flattery of his words. Spinning in his arms, she stared up at him, her hands traveling to the button of his jeans. "How about I see if that feeling is mutual?"

Hunter's mouth lowered to hers, and he kissed her soft

and sensually. His lips were eager and hungry, but his hands reached out to stop hers. "No," he said firmly, his lips still grazing hers.

Gwen's eyebrows rose, but Hunter had her pinned too tightly against him for her to take a step back to look at him in confusion.

He chuckled into her mouth as his hands slid around her back to the clasp of her bra. "Women are fun to stare at when they're naked. Men aren't. We're all dangly parts and big feet."

As her bra came off, Gwen asked in an indignant voice, "So you get to stare at me all naked, but I don't get to look at you?"

Hunter hefted one of her breasts in his hand, testing the weight and size of it. "Precisely," he answered. Seemingly pleased with her breast, he reached up to cup the other one, stroking them both with his thumbs. "Besides, you saw me naked the first day we met. I am sure that was long enough to assess anything you might be curious about. No need to put you through that again."

Gwen closed her eyes at the sensation and gave a little hiss of delight. That didn't stop her from arguing, "But you're so pretty! Your skin's all tan, and you're tall! I look like a ghost. My skin is practically transparent. I'm sure you're more attractive to look at than me."

Letting his hands drop away from her breasts, Hunter trailed them down her stomach. "I would be annoyed right now if I wasn't so certain you weren't fishing for a compliment." His fingers hooked into the waistband of her panties. "Your skin is like alabaster. You're perfect and creamy, like a porcelain doll." His lips curved in amusement. "My little Gwen doll." He squatted, sliding her panties down. As he did, he left a gentle kiss against her hip. When he stood to face her, she was naked and exposed. "Like I said, you're perfect."

Gwen went to protest, but he pressed a finger to her lips. "If I didn't believe that, would I be so happy to have you naked?" he asked, grabbing one of her hands to press it to the bulge in the front of his jeans.

Gwen felt a spark race through her body, and this time it had nothing to do with elf magic. She stroked her hand along the strained fabric. Her bottom lip caught between her teeth as her heart, which normally didn't even beat, gave a thump of excitement.

Leaving her hand where it was, Hunter began running his fingertips over her skin. He caressed and massaged, teasing her with his skilled fingers. He was very careful to avoid her most sensitive areas, working her into a frenzy of need by purposefully avoiding the places she wanted touched the most.

"Hunter," she grumbled, still stroking him through his jeans. "You're not being very nice."

"I don't know what you mean," he lied. He finally conceded enough to run his thumb along one of her nipples.

Gwen gasped and arched into his hand. "If you aren't inside of me within the next two minutes, I'm going to break something else on you."

Hunter merely chuckled at her threat. "I like the fact that you're so dangerous. It makes this all the more enticing." Scooping her up, he wrapped her legs around his waist. He paused for a moment, giving a groan at the feel of having her pressed so intimately against him. Recovering quickly, he dropped her to the bed, placing himself between her knees. "*Now* I'll get undressed. How could I not with such threats hanging over my head?"

Eyes sparking with eagerness, Gwen watched in fascination as Hunter pulled his shirt over his head and tossed it behind him to the floor. "Hot damn," she exclaimed, taking in his ridiculously nice abs.

Hunter grinned, his expression smug.

Gwen reached up to grab the waistband of his jeans. She wrapped her fist around the fabric and yanked him down to her, her mouth on his the instant he was close enough.

He braced himself on his forearm, chuckling into her mouth. "And here I thought you'd never warm up to me," he mumbled between kisses.

Ignoring his comment, Gwen frantically fumbled with the button of his jeans. She'd never wanted anyone so much in her life as she did the man before her. Something about Hunter called to her. The mere touch of his skin on hers had her body thrumming with desire like she'd never felt before.

She gave a cry of triumph when she managed to get the zipper of his jeans down. Without warning, she plunged her hand inside, under his boxers, to grip him in her fist, her fingers firm on his soft flesh.

Hunter groaned and squirmed to get his pants and boxers over his hips.

Gwen didn't wait for him to get them any further. She guided his thick length toward her, guiding him inside of her. He made a strangled choking sound in the back of his throat and flexed his hips to slide himself deeper inside of her. He seemingly forgot or didn't see a need to remove his pants the rest of the way. They stayed low on his thighs, rubbing against the inside of hers.

She slid her legs up and around his hips and arched her own off the bed. "Hard," she begged, making her request simple and to the point.

Hunter bobbed his head in agreement. "That sounds about right."

As he forced himself roughly into her, Gwen threw all her gentle elf stereotypes out the window. He did exactly as she requested, his movements rough and hard. He had her climax approaching so swiftly it had her nearly seeing stars.

"Now. Now," Gwen panted as he thrust and pounded into her. The headboard cracked against the wall as pleasure slammed through her, drawing a ragged cry from her throat.

Hunter reached his own fulfillment at the same time. He groaned into her ear, clutching a fistful of her hair between his fingers.

They laid in silence, the only noise being Hunter's ragged gasps for air. Gwen liked that sound. Not only was it comforting, it let her know he must have enjoyed himself as much as she had. Her body was still trembling around his, her legs quaking from the intensity of her release.

"Wow," Hunter breathed a moment later when he could finally catch his breath. "I'd planned on going the romantic, gentle route, but I think this may have worked out better."

"It was perfect," Gwen reassured. In a move that surprised her, she hooked her legs behind Hunter's back to keep him pinned against her. "Really, really perfect." She was normally the type to bolt after sex, so it was really a surprise to her that she was holding him in place.

Hunter's hand ran gently through her hair. "Glad to hear that," he whispered as he lowered his mouth down to hers for a gentle kiss.

She sighed in contentment and let her eyes slip closed. She could feel Hunter's lips curve into a smile against her own.

"We've got some serious chemistry, little lady. Don't tell me you can't feel it."

"Mmm," she mumbled when he nibbled along her jaw. "I feel it. Always have. I just hated to admit that I was so attracted to a damn elf."

He laughed, obviously not offended by her statement. "I agree. It is hard to believe. I never would have thought that I would have the most amazing sex of my life with a vampire."

He moved away to remove his jeans, and Gwen let him. "This is quite a predicament," she commented. "What do you suppose we do about this?"

Once free of his clothing, Hunter lowered himself to lie next to her. He wrapped an arm around her, pulling her in toward his chest. "We don't have much choice, do we? Fate has brought us together to have amazing sex and annoy the hell out of each other. Our only option is to succumb and enjoy the benefits."

"So it's fate then?" she asked, her voice full of humor. Her arm slid around his thin waist, and her fingertips caressed his hip. "We're just supposed to accept it?"

"Yep."

She placed her head on his shoulder, nuzzling against his throat. "I'm not the relationship type of girl," she warned.

"I'm not the *save the world, battle against evil* type of guy," he responded.

Gwen lay in silence for a moment, thinking that over. Finally, she said, "I like you anyway."

Hunter chuckled and hugged her tightly to him. "I like you anyway too."

With a smile, Gwen closed her eyes and drifted off to sleep. It wasn't until hours later when she awoke that she looked at the clock and cursed. She untangled herself from Hunters arms, moving as quietly as possible so she wouldn't wake him. She slipped into her clothes, silently thanking her good night vision for helping her find them.

She was just pulling her pants over her hips when Hunter's groggy voice broke through the silence. "Where are you going?"

Gwen cringed. "Sorry. I was trying not to wake you," she apologized. "I have to run home."

One of his eyes peeked open, and he held her in his emerald gaze. "You coming back?"

She had to pause to think on that. "Yeah...yeah, I believe I am." Her tone was a mixture of surprise and delight.

"Good. The bed gets too warm without your chilly toes to cool me off." He patted the bed next to him, motioning for her to join him before she left.

She only hesitated a moment before making her way over to the bed.

Instead of letting her sit next to him, Hunter pulled her down to straddle his waist. "I hate to pry into your business, but this isn't a dangerous trip, is it?"

"No you don't, and no it's not." He still looked concerned, so she felt compelled to add, "Colton was supposed to call my cell phone to let me know he'd gotten safely out of town. I left my cell phone at my place. I'm just going to get it and come right back."

"You want me to go with?" Hunter offered with a sleep-filled yawn.

She couldn't help but smile affectionately. "No. You get some sleep. I'll be right back in twenty minutes."

"You sure?"

"Positive."

He looked like he was about to argue, but then changed his mind. "Before you go, can I get a little sugar?" he drawled.

Gwen narrowed her eyes but ended up giving in and laughing. With a mock huff of annoyance, she bent over him. Her hands went to his cheeks, and she kissed him ever so gently. The kiss, which she'd meant to be quick, continued on and on. She heard the comforter rustle with Hunter's movement, and then suddenly his arms were around her waist.

He deepened the kiss, nudging her mouth open with his.

Making a noise of pleasure, she leaned closer to him, letting her hips shift suggestively against him.

"You'd better hurry back, Gwenny," Hunter advised, "because I am fully prepared to give you wake-up sex." He nibbled on her lower lip for a second. "I'm feeling a little kinky. You just might be able to convince me to let you feed off me while we do it," he said teasingly. He actually wasn't quite sure how he felt about being vampire food. It was something he'd never even considered, but suddenly the contemplation was planted in his mind.

Gwen made a soft noise of delight at that thought. There was nothing better than mixing blood with sex. Sex with Hunter was the best she'd ever experienced to begin with. Add blood to that, and she might die of pleasure. She groaned in disappointment as she pulled away from him, knowing she had to. "You sure do give a girl incentive to return."

"That was the idea," he replied, giving her a playful slap across the backside as she climbed to her feet. "See you in twenty."

She nodded agreement as she slipped into the hallway. "Twenty," she promised.

Chapter 9

Hunter's car screeched to a halt in front of Gwen's apartment building. He threw it into park, not caring that he was taking up three different parking spaces. His pulse hammering against his rib cage, he raced up the steps to the front door. The frantic beat of his heart nearly stopped. Then his pulse thudded erratically in his chest at discovering the door hanging partly open. That wasn't a good sign.

He'd awoken four hours after Gwen left, cold and alone. He'd thought for a second she was blowing him off, but the nagging sensation in his gut told him otherwise. Something was wrong.

He entered the building without waiting for an invitation and shut the door behind him. "Gwen!" he hollered, not caring who heard him. "Are you here?" Silence answered him. He bound up the stairs to the second floor where Gwen's living area was. The instant his foot hit the landing, his stomach tightened in dread.

There were thin streaks of blood along the wall that looked like they'd been left behind by fingers, and the wallpaper was scraped back as if someone had been clawing at it to keep from being pulled down the stairs. His stomach turned at the thought of Gwen being dragged down those steps. Just because she was a vampire and durable didn't mean she didn't feel pain.

Hunter followed the trail of blood past an overturned table and a busted lamp. There'd obviously been a struggle. It pained him to know his supposition was correct. He would almost rather have her be ditching him than to be bleeding and in danger.

On the floor in the doorway to Gwen's bedroom lay her cell phone. Hunter bent to pick it up and froze with a sharp intake of air. There were three bullet holes in the wall near Gwen's vanity table. Blood caked the white surface and splattered the floor. It caused his own blood to run cold at the sight. Without entering the room to do any further investigating, Hunter turned and raced back down the stairs. "What did they do to you, Gwenny?" he asked under his breath.

Upon turning the corner of the landing, he ran face first into Colton's broad chest. "We have to do something!" he told the vampire with desperation, not even bothering to feel embarrassed at nearly being knocked over by their collision.

Colton, the much bigger man, didn't even budge when Hunter slammed into him. "Do what?" His brow furrowed in confusion as he peered at Hunter. "And why are you here?"

"Gwen's missing. We have to save her," Hunter rushed out breathlessly.

"I'm sure Gwen's fine," Colton assured, not looking concerned in the least about his friend's well being. "I talked to her a couple hours ago when she got in."

"Well something happened to her after that!" Hunter cried, voice frantic. "She said she'd come back to my place after she talked with you. She never did."

A dawning of realization flitted across Colton's face. A moment later, a look of pity replaced it. "Um...the thing is..." he sighed, running a hand along the back of his neck, looking uncomfortable with the conversation. "See, Gwen isn't exactly the morning after type. She probably just took off. It's kind of her thing."

"This isn't her running off after sex! Something's happened!" Hunter yelled. Every second that ticked by without Colton believing him was a second closer to Mario murdering Gwen. He hated the thought of wasting even a moment on explanations. "There is blood all over her bedroom! I don't think she faked her own abduction to get me to back off."

Colton's expression turned to genuine alarm, and finally he seemed to be listening to Hunter. "Blood?"

"Yeah. And bullet holes in the wall. I...I think she got shot." Hunter was suddenly very thankful that Gwen was a vampire. She wouldn't bleed to death, and a bullet wound couldn't kill her.

"Shit," Colton snarled under his breath. "They retaliated much quicker than we'd expected. We figured we would have at least a few days to figure out a security plan."

A tired looking Penny stepped out from behind her boyfriend, her large elf eyes wide in concern. An overnight bag was slung across her arm. It appeared as if they had just gotten back home from escorting the Wilson family out of town. "Colton, you have to do something," she informed him. She chewed nervously at the sleeve of her shirt, nibbling the fabric at her wrist.

Glancing down at her, Colton hesitated only a moment. "You're right. We'll just have to break back into Cessarini's." His gaze swept to Hunter, and cautiously, he said, "I don't have the money readily available to pay you to go in a second time."

"I don't care about the money," Hunter said, appalled Colton could believe him to be that coldhearted. "What I care about is getting Gwen out of there."

Colton nodded, his expression one of relief. "Good. Keep in mind though, this isn't a sneak and grab mission anymore. I'm going in there with the intent to kill. Mario won't stop until he's dead. If you aren't okay with that, you shouldn't go with me."

"I'm going," Hunter assured him, voice gruff with agitation that Colton would even think he might back out. He didn't care who they had to kill as long as he got Gwen back in one piece. That's all that mattered.

Colton nodded again, accepting his answer. Nudging Hunter with his arm, he motioned for the elf to follow him. "If we're going in, we're going to need weapons. Forget the easily accessible shit we have on hand. I'm unlocking the best we've got." When they reached the first floor apartment, the one renovated into a shared living area, he strode with determination to a small room. After punching in a complex code Hunter was sure he could have gotten anyway, Colton led him inside the room.

Hunter's mouth dropped open in disbelief at the sight in front of him. The entire room was nothing but weapons. Shelves upon shelves were lined with every type of weapon known to man. There were some things he didn't even have a name for, but just by appearance, he knew they were deadly. His eyes lit with eagerness as Colton picked up some sort of machine gun. His expression quickly turned sour, however, when Colton next grabbed a bow and arrow set and handed it over. "What the hell is this?" he asked in bewilderment.

"A bow," Colton replied, looking just as confused at Hunter's question.

"Yes. I see that, but why?" Hunter asked as he turned the contraption over in his hands to examine it. "Who do you think I am, freaking Robin Hood?"

"You're an elf," Colton said in puzzlement. "That's what you guys use."

Penny, who had followed them into the room, swatted her boyfriend in the chest at his stereotype of her people.

"A bow?" Hunter asked in disbelief. "You think I use a bow?" He snorted at the idea, too shocked to be offended. "When and where? Do you think when carburetors are being tricky, I whip out the old bow and arrow?" Before the vampire could respond, he snapped, "Give me a gun! At least those seem pretty self-explanatory. Point, shoot. Easy enough."

Reluctantly, Colton lifted a gun that matched his own. "This is the most beautiful weapon in our collection. It is easy to shoot and will tear the shit out of whatever you're aiming at. This one belongs to Gwen. It's her absolute favorite for situations like this. She never lets anyone else touch it. She didn't even let me use it the time I jammed mine up and begged to borrow hers. Point being, she's very territorial over her weapons, but I'm sure under the circumstances..."

"I'm sure she won't mind." Hunter took the gun from him, feeling slightly alarmed that there had been other circumstances like this before. He, personally, could count on one finger how many times he'd felt the need to use a machine gun. Today.

When Hunter went to hand back the bow, Colton held a hand up to stop him. "Keep it on you. You never know when it might come in handy, and I'd feel better knowing you had it."

Hunter's eyebrows furrowed in skepticism as he surveyed the bow and its quiver full of arrows. "I am not dying with this thing strapped across my back. That's a far too shameful way to go."

Colton scowled. "I'd feel better if you just brought it anyway. Even if you never use it, at least the option is there." After a beat, he went for the guilt angle. "For Gwen," he added.

With a long-suffering sigh, Hunter slid his arm through the hole that would strap everything across his back. "I don't see you packing a bunch of crosses and holy water," he grumbled.

Colton let out a booming, amused laugh, unable to stop his reaction despite the gravity of their situation. "I'm a vampire. If we were going by stereotypes, I would be avoiding those things, not bringing them as weapons."

"Whatever," was the mumbled response.

Shaking his head with a chuckle, Colton clapped Hunter on the shoulder and said, "Alright, Robin Hood, let's go."

Chapter 10

Hunter stared through the windshield of Colton's truck at the gate of Mario Cessarini's home. Back at the apartment, he'd been all tough resolve and murderous intentions, but now that he could see their goal in front of them, his stomach was in knots. He wasn't a killer. It wasn't in his nature. His actions over the next few hours would go against all that, and he knew it. He accepted it, but he was still frightened over what he knew he was going to have to do.

Colton, in the driver seat, revved the engine. "You ready for this, elf?" he asked, though he didn't sound as if he expected an answer. He revved the engine again, the noise echoing through the quiet night. "You better have that gun ready, because we aren't going in all stealth like you and Gwen did." His lips curved into a devilish grin. "I don't do stealth." With that, his foot slammed down onto the gas pedal.

The truck sped toward the iron gate, and Hunter barely had enough time to grab onto the armrest before they crashed through.

"Think they know we're here?" Colton asked in amusement as he swung himself out of the truck. The front door of the mansion flew open, and he opened fire with his machine gun on the first werewolf through.

The man who had been unlucky enough to come through the door first jerked as bullets riddled his body. He fell to the ground. His head lolled, and his eyes stared lifelessly out at them. The others behind him ducked back inside, more wary than they'd originally been.

"Like vampires, they're hard to kill," Colton instructed. "Even harder in wolf form, but it can be done. Aim for the heart or the brain. Anything else will merely slow them down and piss them off."

Hunter climbed out of the truck reluctantly, his hands trembling. He picked up his gun, Gwen's gun, and wondered not for the first time what he was doing. He was a mechanic! What was he doing with a gun? What was he doing taking on an aggressive werewolf pack?

In the heartbeat in which he second-guessed himself, four werewolves poured out of the mansion's front door. They'd shifted to animal form, and now their paws pounded down the drive toward the wrecked gate, their jaws snapping with fury.

Colton never hesitated. He fired immediately at the oncoming group.

Hunter backtracked away from them, his heart racing. He didn't want to kill, not again. He was hoping to be able to stay back and let Colton handle the group. After all, his main goal was to heal Gwen's bullet wounds, not fight. His hope of this was soon dashed when one of the wolves got past Colton.

It made a beeline for Hunter, determination evident in every heavy footfall. The werewolf crouched and sprang, teeth aimed for his jugular.

Hunter stumbled backwards, his finger hesitating on the trigger. It wasn't until the werewolf was inches from him that he finally pulled the trigger. He had no choice. He fired, and the spray of bullets tore into the werewolf's chest.

The wolf collapsed at his feet with a shrill yap of agony before going still.

Hunter let out a whoosh of air. "Shit," he whispered, bending at the waist to put his hands on his knees in hopes of calming his frantically beating heart.

"Don't kill often?" Colton asked. His voice held amusement, but there was an underlying tone of pity.

"Just once before," Hunter admitted. "I knew the man I killed. I knew he deserved it." He nodded to the werewolf on the ground in front of him who was shifting back to human form in death. "I don't even know this guy. How do I know whether he deserved this?"

"He did," was Colton's unruffled response. "All these wolves who are rushing at us are Mario's thugs. These are the ones who egg on his behavior. The lower members of this pack are used to being kicked around. They'll cower, not attack. Rest assured, any of the men who rush out here to attack us are guilty. Any of Gwen's blood that has been spilled is on their hands as well as Mario's."

Hunter was familiar with this werewolf pack enough to know Colton was right when he mentioned the lower members of the pack being docile. They were afraid to stand up for themselves, afraid to even run. Mario had such a tight leash on them, half were terrified of their own shadows. He nodded, his reluctance fading away at the truth in the vampire's statement. "Gwen had better still be alive, or I will kill every last one of Mario's thugs."

"Agreed."

With new resolve, Hunter followed Colton as he marched purposefully toward the open front door. There were already five dead werewolves on the lawn. He wondered how many more bodies there would be before the night was out.

At the door, Colton became more cautious. He stepped into the expansive foyer, not even making a sound. "You know where the holding cells are located," he whispered as his feet silently moved him farther into the room. "Lead the way. I've got you covered."

Hunter nodded and started down the hallway to his left, trying to get a feel from the building with his magic as to Gwen's exact location. Last time, he and Gwen had entered from a different part of the house, but he still felt he could find his way to her without much trouble now.

Colton fell into step behind him, his eyes darting warily into open doorways. He never let Hunter get more than a few steps ahead of him. Without the elf, he'd never be able to get Gwen out of her holding cell. He was next to useless when it came to electronics.

Hunter pressed on, unable to hear anything around the frantic pounding of his own heart. When a pair of eyes stared at him from the darkness of a room he passed, he thought he might have a heart attack on the spot.

"I told you the more submissive members wouldn't attack," Colton assured, obviously having seen Hunter's hesitation to move past the peering person hidden in the darkness.

"You're safe from them. Keep moving."

They passed the next doorway and were nearly clear of danger when Colton reached out and grabbed Hunter by the collar of his leather jacket. He shoved the elf behind him and was already raising his gun when a werewolf lunged into the hallway. It scrambled to quickly face them, a low snarl escaping between a vicious set of teeth.

"I know you understand me," Colton reasoned, not wanting to shoot until the werewolf attacked. "I'm offering you a chance to walk away. We're leaving here with my girl. Do you really want to die just to give your boss a couple extra minutes before he starts a hostage negotiation?"

The werewolf growled again, shifting on his haunches as if prepared to spring.

Colton never gave him the opportunity. "Your choice." He pulled the trigger of his gun. Bullets sprayed, the majority of them lodging inside the werewolf's skull. Blood pelted the wall, flying with enough force to splatter.

Hunter had a hard time keeping last night's dinner down. He swallowed roughly, trying to keep his gaze from straying to the gore that now littered the carpet. On Colton's grunted order, he stumbled past the body, moaning when something squished underneath him as he walked. He tried not to picture gray brain matter being ground into the carpet, but the sensation of it under his shoes made it nearly impossible to suppress the image.

At the next doorway, half a dozen away from the holding cells, stood another man. He was tall and lean with dark black hair that fell across his forehead. His shoulders were bunched with tension and an inhuman growl rumbled in his chest.

Colton stepped into the man's path, taking an intimidating stance in front of him. "It's not worth it."

The man started to growl again when a petite Hispanic woman rushed forward and grabbed his arms. "Milo, no," she pleaded. Her rich, chocolate brown eyes lifted to Colton's, and she gazed at him through a wave of thick, waist length hair that had cascaded over her shoulder. "Please," she directed at Colton. "This is not our fight. We do not support Mario's wicked acts."

"Then don't die for them either," Colton advised.

Milo continued to glare, but the growling in his chest subsided, and he took a step back.

The girl looked imploringly into Colton's eyes when she was sure the man with her was going to back down. "Kill them all," she breathed.

"Raina!" Milo scolded, his tone aghast.

Raina's eyes stayed calm, unconcerned with his shock. "You could lead us better, brother. You're strong enough."

"You might just get a chance to find out," Colton informed him. With that, he continued down the hallway.

As they reached the doors that were used to hold people prisoner, Colton motioned to one that was slightly ajar. Jeers of cruel delight could be heard from within. With a sneer of disgust, he said, "I'm betting that's our door."

Hunter bobbed his head once, too nervous to do anything more. It appeared as if his ability to get into locked doors wouldn't be needed. Good. That meant he could concentrate all his efforts on Gwen. Following after Colton, he crept toward the room.

Once there, he expected them to sneak up on Gwen's abductors, but Colton kicked the door open, busting the top hinge.

Eyes widening in surprise, Hunter scurried after Colton, entering the room on the heels of the furious vampire. There was instant chaos upon their arrival, and through the scrambling bodies, he could see a fragile form sprawled on a bed against the wall.

As his brain recognized the still form as Gwen, Hunter pushed all else out of his thoughts. While Colton fought against the half dozen men in the room, he made a beeline for Gwen.

Someone reached out and grabbed onto his arm, trying to keep him from getting across the room.

Hunter swung his gun around, cracking the werewolf in the nose with it. He heard the satisfying sound of breaking bone but didn't stop to check out the damage he'd done. He kept moving toward Gwen.

He could see her lip was busted and blood glossed across it. Her right arm seemed to be broken. At best, she was unconscious. At worst...well, he didn't even want to think about that option.

As he reached her side, he noticed her knuckles were

bruised and bloodied. She'd gone down swinging. He was filled with pride at knowing she'd fought back. Dropping to his knees next to the bed, he saw the bullet wounds. Two were in her right shoulder, one by her hip. Grabbing her wrist, Hunter frantically felt for a pulse. His heart was just seizing in terror when he remembered she was a vampire. No pulse.

Ignoring the sounds of the fight behind him, Hunter slid his hands gently around her neck, his thumbs grazing along her chin. "Gwenny, wake up." He gently moved her head from side to side, attempting to rouse her. "Damn it. Be okay!"

A gun fired in the background, but he didn't have time to turn and check on Colton, because Gwen's eyelashes finally fluttered open. It took her a moment to orient herself, and then she rasped out, "Hunter?" Her blue eyes filled with relief. "You came looking for me."

"Of course I came looking for you," he said, sounding slightly offended there'd been any doubt. "I love you. How could I not do everything in my power to get you back?"

Though she was exhausted and in pain, Gwen managed a small smile. "You are the most amazing man I've ever met." She rolled her eyes playfully. "I finally find a decent guy, and he's an elf. Go figure."

"We all have our crosses to bear," he said with a smile in return. He brushed her hair away from her forehead with his free hand. "How do you think I feel knowing you look at me like I'm just a midnight Wendy's run?"

She went to comment, but instead, her pretty eyes suddenly widened in surprise at something behind Hunter. Before she could say anything, the gun in Hunter's hand was ripped away. It went skittering across the floor out of his reach.

Mario Cessarini stepped between the gun and its owner. "You've caused some real trouble for me." His expression turned to shock when he recognized Hunter. "You!" he accused. His hands balled into fists, and he took a menacing step toward them. "I knew I shouldn't have let you walk away the last time. Look at what being merciful gets me, an ungrateful crook!"

"I'm not a crook," Hunter said through clenched teeth. "I just want Gwen. That's all." He climbed to his feet to face

Mario, putting himself between Gwen and the murderous werewolf.

Mario's lip curled into a sneer as he slid a gun from the waistband of his pants. "The two of you can die together. Does that make you happy?"

As Mario aimed the weapon at Hunter, Gwen's hand lifted, and she held it out pleadingly. "No," she begged, struggling to get to a half-sitting position, using the headboard of the bed against her back to hold herself up.

Hunter began moving backwards and away from Gwen. If the gun was pointed at him, he didn't want to be standing in front of her. He held his hands up, placating, though he knew it would do him no good. He just wanted to get a little bit of space between them before...

As Mario pulled the trigger, Hunter barely managed to dive behind a thick oak table to his right. The corner of the table shattered into shards as a bullet tore through it.

Hunter rolled, moving further behind the table, and putting his back to the wall. In a quick movement, he tipped the heavy oak table over, giving himself some cover from the homicidal werewolf. "Shit, shit, shit," he cursed under his breath. He was weaponless and under fire. He looked frantically to both sides of him for something, anything he could possibly use as a weapon. As he moved, he jerked in surprise as something dug into his back. It was that damn bow and arrow Colton forced him to bring.

Hands trembling with nerves, he undid the strap that was holding the bow across his back. It was better than nothing, he presumed. Reaching over his shoulder, he pulled one of the arrows from the quiver, feeling downright foolish. He'd never used one of these before in his life. What made him think he'd be able to learn now while worrying about the crazed werewolf shooting at him with a gun? He struggled to get the arrow in position. After dropping it to the floor on his first two attempts, he finally managed to get the arrow into place.

Springing to his feet, Hunter took aim at Mario. When he let go of the arrow, it went a few feet, hit the ground, and skidded uselessly across the linoleum floor. "Damn!" he hissed, ducking back down to hide behind the overturned table. When standing, he'd seen Colton occupied in hand-to-hand combat with Chrispen Winthrow. Hunter was on his own.

"What is this?" Mario's voice asked tauntingly from the other side of the table. "An arrow? Oh, now I've seen everything." He inhaled deeply, and then let his breath out with a delighted huff. "I can smell the fear on you, boy."

Hunter could hear him moving close. His mind pictured the werewolf inching closer, his gun raised and aimed, ready for the next time Hunter stood.

"Do you know what a werewolf likes to do when he senses fear?" Mario asked conversationally. "Fear makes us go a little crazy. Even those of us who are best at self-restraint have trouble holding back when we have our prey cornered and shaking with fear."

Hunter heard him kick the arrow out of the way, putting him at less than ten feet away.

"When a werewolf senses fear, he likes to tear out his victim's throat. Our teeth are perfect for that, you know? They can tear through meat better than any other predator out there. How would you like to die, boy? Would you prefer the gun, or would you rather die like a man and have me do you with my teeth?"

Taking a deep, shuddering breath, Hunter grabbed another arrow, cursing himself for never getting in touch with his heritage. He jammed it into place, and before he could even think about how unlikely he was to succeed against a gun, he lunged to his feet.

The second he was in view, Mario fired.

Hunter turned his side to the werewolf, taking the bullet in the shoulder. With a hiss of pain, he swung the bow around and let go of the arrow.

He heard the dull thud before his eyes registered what happened.

Mario was clutching at the wooden stem of the arrow that was sticking out of his chest. He collapsed to his knees, looking shocked. "How?" he asked in disbelief. "Impossible..."

As Hunter watched the life drain from Mario's eyes, he gave a surprised bark of laughter. "The bow actually worked. Hot damn, Colton is a genius." Ignoring the pain in his shoulder, he raced over to the bed and dropped to his knees in front of Gwen. Glancing over his shoulder, he saw Chrispen staring at Mario's body in utter shock.

This distraction was all Colton needed. He grabbed Chrispen's head and twisted violently, snapping bones vital to even a werewolf's continued existence. With a nod to Hunter, he dropped the body to the floor.

Hunter couldn't believe it. They'd done it. They'd stopped Mario from killing Gwen. And without the loss of either of their lives!

"I still can't believe you're here," Gwen whispered, bringing Hunter's attention back to her. Her voice was thick with pain, and she gently lowered herself back down to the bed now that the violence was over.

"Believe it," Hunter came back. "You knew Colton and I would never have let Mario kill you." He brushed her hair away from her face, surveying her injuries. "What hurts the most?" he asked, changing the subject from the dead werewolf to the wounds of the woman in front of him.

"My pride?" she replied with a wry grin.

Rolling his eyes, he reached out and grabbed her broken arm. He gripped it tightly between both of his hands. "This is going to hurt." In one swift movement, he reset the bone, not giving her time to think on it. He cringed at her holler of pain, but concentrated on sending healing power into the damage.

Her skin glowed as bone knitted back together, healing in moments what would take a human months to achieve naturally.

Once he was pleased with the shape of her arm, he moved his fingers to the bullet wounds. "You aren't going to like this," he warned. "I have to get the bullets out before I can heal these."

Her face pale, Gwen gritted her teeth and nodded. "Just do it." She motioned toward a cabinet along the wall. "There are knives in there."

"How do you know?" Hunter asked, though the second the question was out of his mouth, he regretted it. He had a good guess at how she knew.

Gwen grimaced, her gaze flicking to deep slashes at her wrists, confirming his assumption. "Trust me. I know."

Hunter had been so intent on her broken arm and bullet wounds when he found her that he'd missed her wrists. "My God," he breathed when she drew his attention to them. He gently lifted one of her wrists into his palm.

Behind him, Colton rifled through the cabinet Gwen had

pointed to for a knife.

While he waited for Colton to join them, Hunter fearfully wondered what other injuries he'd skimmed over in his haste. His gaze slid to hers and he asked, "They didn't..." He trailed off, unable to voice the horrible place his mind wandered.

Knowing Hunter was fearful she'd been sexually violated, Gwen quickly shook her head to ease his fears. "No. They didn't do anything else to me other than the few things you see here. The bullet wounds happened in my apartment, the broken arm when they brought me into the building. I fought back instead of being a compliant little hostage. I broke someone's face, and they broke my arm in return."

Hunter healed the gashes in her wrists while he listened, stroking his fingers tenderly along her torn flesh, hating these men all over again.

Gwen glanced down at her glowing wrist with amusement. "You don't have to do that. Vampire's heal fast."

"Not as fast as I can heal you," Hunter grumbled, moving on to her other wrist.

She shrugged, though a pleased smile touched her lips. "Anyway," she continued, "when I got into this room, they let me be for awhile. I think they were hoping I'd go a little crazy with fear. When they realized that wasn't going to happen anytime soon, they came in and sliced my wrists up pretty good. I must have lost consciousness from lack of blood, because that is the last thing I remember before seeing you."

Hunter breathed a sigh of relief, releasing Gwen's wrists as Colton made his way over to them.

The other man handed over a sharp, vicious looking knife. "Get it done," he said gruffly.

Hunter took the knife in silence, his stomach roiling at the thought of what he was about to do. "I'm sorry," he apologized in advance. Gripping the knife, he forced his hands to stay steady. He started with her hip. Taking a deep breath, he dug the knife into her skin. He pried into the wound until he managed to get the bullet to the surface.

Gwen made a soft noise of pain, her hands clenching into fists.

As soon as the bullet was free, he placed his hands to the newly bleeding wound and forced it to heal. He watched the tension ease out of her face when the skin was new and bullet free. It was the only thing that gave him the strength to dig out the other two bullets. Moving as quickly as possible, he repeated the procedure with each bullet hole, wanting nothing more than to alleviate her pain. When he finished, Hunter's forehead was covered in a nervous sweat. He felt better though, knowing Gwen was going to be fine.

His relief wasn't long-lived before Colton said, "She needs blood. She's lost too much." He cursed under his breath. "We're nearly out at home. We've been meaning to refill our stock, but Dr. Wilson is the one who usually supplies us with blood. The nearest blood bank is over fifty miles away, and she needs blood now. Also, we would need to steal—"

Making a rash decision, Hunter cut him off. "She's not going to a blood bank." Before he could talk himself out of it, he took the knife and turned it to his own wrist. He sliced open his skin, trying not to feel queasy as blood rushed to the surface. With a determined expression, he shoved his bleeding wrist toward Gwen. "Drink," he instructed.

She hesitated, her eyes searching his face for reluctance or perhaps even disgust.

Hunter knew that most people found a vampire's eating habits to be repulsive. He figured she was afraid she'd scare him off if he saw her feed. It didn't matter what she did, that was never going to happen. "I'm losing the blood anyway," he informed her as it slid down onto the edge of his palm. "You might as well make use of it."

He saw the decision in her eyes, and a moment later, Gwen greedily brought his wrist to her mouth.

He cringed at the first scrape of her fangs across his cut wrist but quickly relaxed at the gentle way she sucked the blood escaping it. This wasn't at all how he'd pictured vampires drinking. His imagination had been cruel and emotionless. This...well, this was almost enjoyable.

Colton's voice drew him out of his revelation. "You didn't need to slit your wrist. We have fangs. It is less painful if you let us puncture the skin ourselves."

"Had I done that," Hunter replied calmly, "she never would have done this. She wouldn't have accepted this unless I was already bleeding."

Colton gave him a nod that held respect and gratitude. "You're probably right." He took a step away from them toward the door. "I'll be in the hallway watching out for any more of Mario's henchmen, though the rest have all probably tucked tail and run. You two can join me when you've finished."

Hunter nodded distractedly as he watched Gwen.

She was bent over his arm with her long hair cascading around her shoulders. Even in her wounded state, she lapped and sucked almost sensually at his cut wrist, being careful not to cause any pain.

Watching her bent over him like that was quite likely the most erotic thing he'd ever seen. When things were no longer hectic and they were behind closed bedroom doors, he might just have to explore this feeding thing. He'd said it to her earlier in a moment of passion but hadn't been quite sure if he'd meant it. At this moment, the idea held real appeal.

Her blue eyes suddenly lifted to his, and she halted her movements. She sat back, her eyes watching him intently as she licked her lips clean. "What?" she asked warily.

"I was just thinking about how sexy you look," he admitted, voice low and husky. He gave her a gentle smile as he ran his hand over his wrist, healing the gash he'd made a few moments before.

She laughed softly and shook her head. "You elves don't have a self-preservation bone in your body, do you?"

"Apparently not," he said, tossing her a grin. "If I had any self-preservation at all, I wouldn't have brought my easily breakable self into a house full of pissed off werewolves." As his nerves and hormones settled, he shifted his body and turned the knife to his own skin. He awkwardly dug the bullet out of his shoulder, having a hard time seeing exactly where the entry hole was, although the constant sting in his shoulder was guide enough.

"You got shot?" Gwen asked in surprise, sitting up with a grimace at her obviously sore muscles. "You healed me first," she said in astonishment. "You fed me while you were still injured. Why? Why would you do that?"

The bullet popped loose, and Hunter gave her a soft smile as his skin began healing itself under his hand. "Of course I did. I told you..." He leaned in and kissed her forehead. "I'm crazy about you."

Epilogue

Gwen stood shoulder to shoulder with Hunter at the end of the Wilson family's long driveway. In silence, she observed as Colton helped Marla out of his car, a wide grin spreading across his face at something the young girl said. Content, she let her eyes lift to Hunter's face, taking in the strong line of his jaw for a moment before she pulled an envelope from her inside pocket. "It looks as if things are going to turn out alright. The Wilson's are safe, Colton says Milo is taking over the local pack, and I am not the play thing of sadistic werewolves." She tapped his forearm with the envelope, and then held it out to him. "I'd say you more than held up your end of the bargain."

"What's this?" he asked curiously as he took it from her hands. He turned it over as if looking for an explanation to be written on the back. When he found none, he opened the envelope and glance inside.

"Your hundred thousand," she explained as his eyes widened in shock at the quantity of bills that lay in his palm, sheathed in an unassuming white envelope.

Startling green eyes lifted to hers in surprise. "Gwen..." He shook his head. "I can't possibly take this." He tried giving the envelope back to her, but she refused, pushing it back into his hands.

"You can," she corrected. "You earned it."

"It was never about the money," he argued. "When they took you..." He trailed off as if the memory was too painful. "Things got very personal, especially at the end. I went in there for my own benefit. I wouldn't feel right taking your money."

Gwen closed her hand over his, forcing him to hold on to the envelope. "Keep it. Colton insists. He said to look at it as a retainer."

"A retainer?" Hunter asked with confusion.

"To lock you in as a future consultant when your services are required," Gwen explained in a clipped, business-like tone.

Hunter's eyebrows rose in disbelief. "Future consultant," he repeated as if trying to wrap his brain around the concept. His gaze searched her face, looking for an indication of her feelings on the subject. "How do you feel about that?" he finally asked when he found none.

Gwen shrugged, her face revealing nothing. "Colton's the boss...I suppose. What he says goes, really. If he feels it's safe to put an elf mercenary on the payroll, who am I to question his judgment?"

Hunter shot her a look of mild irritation. "I meant..." His expression grew very serious. "How do you feel about *me* working with you? About me being around, violating your personal space and contaminating it with my elf germs?" He tried to make the statement sound humorous, but it might possibly be one of the most important moments in his life. This was big. If she rejected him, he didn't know what he would do. He'd grown attached to Gwen, grumpy sarcasm and all.

Gwen turned away from his intense gaze. She stared up the drive for a moment in silence, just watching the Wilsons as they unpacked their bags from Colton's car. Finally, without looking at Hunter, she smiled softly. "I think it might be kind of fun." Her face filled with mock seriousness as she added, "Nothing eases the stress of a crazy work day like fornicating with a co-worker. I believe it will really take the edge off."

Hunter grinned widely, his shoulders sagging with relief. Trying not to show just how much the thought of permanently being around excited him, he followed her gaze to the group in front of the house.

Gwen's grin widened as the Wilson family entered their home for the first time since Marla's kidnapping. The sight filled her with a warmth she didn't often feel. The Wilsons were no longer in hiding now that Mario was dead. They were free to return to their lives, living as they'd previously done, without the threat of supernatural menaces. The family had relieved expressions on their faces, though they all looked ragged and drained. It had been a long few days for everyone.

Hunter's arm was suddenly around her shoulder, and he squeezed her affectionately against him. "I see that smile. You aren't as heartless as you pretend to be."

Gwen looked up at him with a noise of delight in the back of her throat as he leaned down and kissed her. "You're making me soft," she accused against his lips.

"And you're making me hard," he teased, his tone thick with the double entendre.

Pulling back, Gwen laughed and slapped a hand playfully against his chest. "Bad elf."

"You love me anyway," he countered.

Her lips quirked at the corners, and she fought a smile, not wanting to encourage him too much. "I might."

Hunter growled and pulled her closer. "Despicable vampire."

Standing on her tiptoes, she nibbled at his chin. "You love me anyway."

Hunter grabbed her face in his hands and gave her an enthusiastic kiss. "Definitely." He grinned wickedly as she curled herself around him, making the darkness of the Wilson's driveway their own private escape from reality.

A few moments later, Colton's head peeked out of the front door of the Wilson home. "Hey! Love birds! This story isn't going to tell itself! Let's go!"

As her best friend ducked back inside the house, Gwen gazed up at Hunter with a question in her eyes. "Are you sure you want to get mixed up with this bunch? There's still time to run."

Hunter gave her another quick kiss, holding her tightly against his chest. "I'm in this pretty deep, Gwenny. I'm ready to make vampire/elf half-breed babies with you." His lips curved into a grin as he continued to tease her. "Though I can only imagine my mother's reaction when she finds out I knocked up a vampire. That is one lecture I don't look forward to."

Rolling her eyes, Gwen pushed away from him and began walking toward the house. "Let's keep it simple, elf boy."

With a laugh, he followed after her. "There is no simple with you, sweetheart, but we can try."

ABOUT THE AUTHOR

Melissa Hosack lives near Pittsburgh, Pennsylvania with her husband Jeremy and their four pets: Duke, Edge, Eddie, and Leia. She writes a monthly short story column titled Frequent Flyer for a government newspaper and had a short story, More Bark Than Bite, published by Mystic Moon Press in September of 2008.

www.ingramcontent.com/pod-product-compliance
Lightning Source LLC
Chambersburg PA
CBHW020630130626
46552CB00003B/1162